GOOD BYE, REBEL BLUE

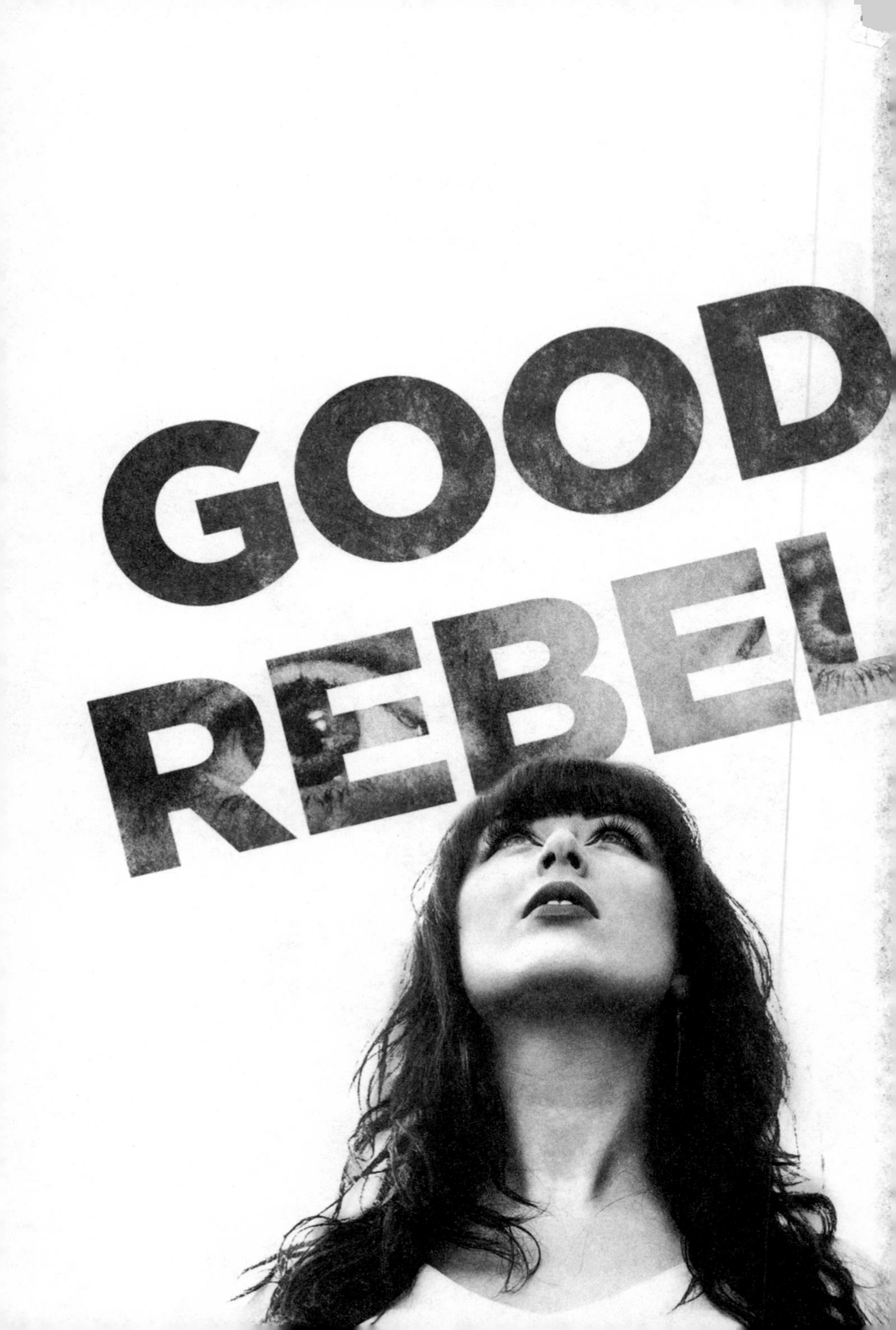
GOOD
REBEL

BYE, BLUE

SHELLEY CORIELL

AMULET BOOKS · NEW YORK

Library of Congress Cataloging-in-Publication Data

Coriell, Shelley.
Goodbye, Rebel Blue / by Shelley Coriell.
  pages cm
Summary: Rebecca "Rebel" Blue, a loner rebel and budding artist, reluctantly completes the bucket list of Kennedy Green, an over-committed do-gooder classmate who dies in a car accident following a stint in detention where both girls were forced to consider their mortality and write bucket lists.
ISBN 978-1-4197-0930-2 (alk. paper)
[1. Conduct of life—Fiction. 2. Self-perception—Fiction. 3. Fate and fatalism—Fiction.] I. Title.
PZ7.C8157Go 2013
[Fic]—dc23
2013010046

Printed and bound in U.S.A.
10 9 8 7 6 5 4 3 2 1

Amulet Books are available at special discounts when purchased in quantity for premiums and promotions as well as fundraising or educational use. Special editions can also be created to specification. For details, contact specialsales@abramsbooks.com or the address below.

115 West 18th Street
New York, NY 10011
www.abramsbooks.com

To the three who died

bucket list (*noun*)—A list of things you want to do before you die; comes from the phrase *kick the bucket* (to die)

CHAPTER
ONE

THE MAKERS OF INSPIRATIONAL KITTY POSTERS should be disemboweled.

The posters cover one wall of the detention room where I sit after school with Macey Kellingsworth and some girl with a perky blond ponytail. Ms. Lungren, one of the Del Rey School's guidance counselors, stands in front of a poster of a fluffy white kitten sitting in a teacup under the words *Everyone needs a daily cup of cuteness.*

I need a puke bucket.

"Each of you received detention today for behavior that can be described as dangerous"—Lungren's eyes bulge—"even deadly."

This morning Lungren caught Macey and me smoking in the girls' bathroom near the auto shop building. "Is that smoke I smell?" Lungren had asked as she burst through the bathroom door, her cat-eye glasses perched on the end of her twitching nose. She spent most mornings prowling about campus searching for bad people doing bad things.

Who was I to disappoint? I puffed out a smoke ring and, with the tip of my finger, slashed through the circle, creating a smoky heart shape. "Consider it a belated valentine."

A ghost of a smile sickled Macey's lips.

Lungren snatched the cigarette from my hand. "Both of you, detention!"

Smoking = Bad. I get that. I took my first drag at age twelve and found the whole process as pleasant as licking soot from a chimney. I would have quit, but it bugged the hell out of Aunt Evelyn, and at age twelve, bugging the hell out of Aunt Evelyn was the only thing I did well.

Four years later, I still puff on the occasional cancer-emphysema-coronary-disease stick, not so much to piss off Aunt Evelyn, but to deal with her. The latest blow: This morning Aunt Evelyn took away my phone and computer privileges. My crime: I failed my Algebra II exam. Aunt Evelyn doesn't get that some people just don't *get* asymptotes.

"A good detention program doesn't punish you," Lungren continues. "Detention *helps* you, gives you the opportunity to examine bad choices and explore ways to improve your lives."

I try to exchange eye rolls with Macey, but she's tugging at the cuffs of her hoodie and staring into Maceyspace. Some brain trust nicknamed Macey the Grim Reaper our freshman year. With her black hoodie, skeletal frame, and pale hair, she looks like death. We met more than two years ago in detention, and while we're hardly best friends, we both like dark places and uncrowded spaces. The other juvenile delinquent in detention today, Ms. Perky Ponytail, darts her gaze around the room as if terrified the kitty will lunge from the teacup and tear apart her flesh. Clearly a detention virgin.

"For the next two hours you will contemplate your inappropriate and potentially deadly behavior," Lungren says.

Perky Ponytail rockets her hand into the air and does one of those *Pick me! Pick me!* waves. She doesn't look like a smoker. I wonder what landed her in kitty hell.

"Yes, Kennedy?" Lungren asks.

"I appreciate what you're doing for me, and I see the long-term value, but I have a 100 Club project this afternoon. Then I need to go to the prom-decorating committee meeting and a fundraiser for endangered leatherback turtles. It's a crazy-busy day. Is it possible to make other arrangements?"

"Someone else will have to save the turtles today," Lungren says, and the girl's ponytail slumps. "Each of you will spend the next two hours thinking about the types of experiences and activities you would choose when faced with the limited time you have on Earth." She waltzes down the aisle and hands us each a cheap spiral notebook. "Here is a brand-new journal, and in here I want you to write things you want to do before you die."

Kennedy raises her hand and waves. "Like a bucket list?"

"You can call it a bucket list or to-do list. The key is to make it thoughtful, make it meaningful, make it you."

Kennedy's hand bolts skyward. *Wave-wave.* "How long does it need to be?"

"As long as you want, but keep in mind, the more time you spend on your list, the deeper you get into your heart."

Macey snorts.

Agreed. What's in my heart is none of a school counselor's business.

Kennedy does the hand thingy again. "Do we turn it in to you when we're done?" Maybe this is her deadly behavior: sucking up to teachers and suffocating them.

"It would be more beneficial for you to keep the list—and the whole journal, for that matter. I've explained to your parents—"

"You talked to my parents?!"

Bad girl, Kennedy—bad, bad girl. You forgot to raise your hand.

"Yes, I talked to your parents and guardians." Lungren looks at me on the last word. "They are aware of your choices and the redirection efforts of this assignment."

Kennedy cradles her cheeks in her palms. "My parents are

going to be so disappointed, and this will go on my school record, and . . ."

Ms. Perky Ponytail needs to reread the poster of the kitty hanging at the end of a rope. You know the one: *Hang in there!* Because Kennedy is lucky she won't have to deal with Aunt Evelyn. As I glare at Lungren, Macey rises from her desk and walks to the door.

"Macey, where are you going?" Without a word, Macey glides into the hall, and Lungren hurries after her, calling over her shoulder, "I'll be right back, girls. Please start your lists."

I yank a pencil stub from my messenger bag. Kennedy sniffles. A drop of body fluid splats on the floor near my right flip-flop. I jerk away. Her shoulders heave. The sniffles grow into choky sobs, and more snorts and snot rush out. Her hands shake.

I glance over my shoulder to the door. Where the hell is Lungren?

Shallow, gaspy sounds fall from Kennedy's mouth. Her face is colorless, bloodless, as if she's about to pass out.

"You know"—I lean across the aisle—"it's not that big of a deal."

"It's . . . it's detention," she says between hiccup-y cries. She sways.

I grab her arm and keep her upright. "And your point?"

She blinks and takes a deep breath.

Good. Breathing is good.

"My parents will k . . . k . . . kill me, my teachers will think I'm turning into a delinquent, my friends won't want to hang out with me, and I won't be class valedictorian next year."

Excellent. She's not dying. She's just a wack job. I let go of her arm. "The only people who will know you're in detention are Lungren, your parents, and yours truly, and I'm not about to broadcast details of this little tea party over the school radio station."

"But—"

"See this?" I jam my notebook under her nose. "The secret to putting this experience behind you is to complete Lungren's assignment. If you don't, she'll have you here tomorrow and every day after until you finish. You need to shut up and write. Just write."

Kennedy opens her notebook. "Write. Just write."

My brilliant wisdom is not lost on me. I, too, need to write a bucket list. Unlike Macey, I can't bolt. I skipped out on detention last month, and Lungren warned me in her singsongy counselor voice, *If you skip another detention, you get a weeklong suspension,* which would not be good for my current math grade. Plus, I'd be forced to stay at home with Aunt Evelyn 24-7, which would not be good for my physical and mental well-being. This time I need to play by the rules.

I snap open the cover of my *journal.* The problem is, I'm not good at rules. A let's-cut-to-the-chase therapist told me years ago that I have problems with rules because I spent the first ten years of my life barefoot. He said if I started wearing shoes, Aunt Evelyn would be in a happier place, she'd stop punishing me so much, and the entire world would make paper cranes instead of nuclear bombs.

And I'm going to be nominated for Mistletoe Queen.

I aim my pencil stub like a pistol at my notebook. *Bucket list* sounds too normal. I lick the tip of my pencil and write, *Goodbye, Rebel Blue.*

A shadow passes over the paper. "Uh, thanks for the advice. I've never been in detention before." Kennedy straddles the chair in front of my desk.

I peek through a streak of blue hair hanging across my face. Her cheeks are no longer bloodless. She isn't going to die in my presence. Therefore, she is no longer my problem.

"I was exaggerating when I said my parents would kill me. They have high expectations, but I'm harder on myself than they are. I want to do things right, you know? Be the best me I can be."

I draw wavy lines and swirls alongside my notebook's spiral.

She places her arms on the chair back and tilts her head. "I'm not sure if you remember, Rebel, but we had art together freshman year."

I add design lines to the top of the page.

"You want to hear something weird?" She edges closer, her ponytail swinging forward and brushing against the top of my desk.

I sketch more squiggles at the bottom of the paper. They look like waves, and I add shells and a starfish. The starfish flips off Kennedy.

"Our freshman year I thought it would be kind of neat if we could be friends. You know, the whole color thing, Rebecca Blue and Kennedy Green. Because—get this—blue-green is my favorite color. Not teal or aqua but blue-green, the world's most perfect color, and here we are again, Blue and Green."

I write the numbers one through twenty down the left side of the page.

"Oh, good! You're starting your bucket list. It's a weird assignment but fascinating. You can learn a lot about people when you know the things they want to do before they die."

I give her the you-are-annoying-the-crap-out-of-me look I reserve for Aunt Evelyn on her I'm-grounding-you-for-life days.

"I think about death sometimes and what happens next. I think people who live good lives on Earth go to good places when they die. Do you ever think about death?"

Yes. Right now.

"My grandmother died while she was having open-heart surgery last year. She flatlined for more than a minute, but the doctors brought her back. She said it was the most incredible sixty seconds of her life. She saw a golden light and a lady in gold and a tunnel with glittery gold bricks. Maybe that's why my heaven is gold." She's so close, I smell her shampoo. Sunshine and citrus. "What color's your heaven?"

Ignoring Kennedy is clearly not working. "Black," I say. "The color of a world six feet under, with hundreds of gray squiggles, which would be worms eating at my decaying corpse."

She draws closer, not repulsed. She should be repulsed. "You don't believe in life after this one? You believe that this"—she waves at the kitty posters—"is all there is?"

"I believe you are a moron."

"I understand." Kennedy uses Lungren's creepy counselor tone. "Talking about death and dying is hard for most people. Some people are afraid of death and what lies beyond."

"I am not afraid of death, because there's nothing beyond death. No feelings, no fear, no me."

Her dopey grin fades away. "What are you afraid of, Rebel? Right here. Right now." Her voice softens, but the sharpness, the brightness in her eyes intensifies. "Don't tell me *nothing*, because everyone's afraid of something." I open my mouth, and she points an arrow-straight finger at my chest. "No lies."

I almost laugh. *Lies?* Not in my world. "I'm afraid of being ordinary."

Her face remains serious. "You, Rebel Blue, are anything but ordinary." She settles her spine against the desk and picks at the back of the chair, flecks of brown paint drifting to the floor like sand. "I'm afraid of spiders and twenty-foot squid and phone calls that come in the middle of the night." She scratches harder, faster. "I'm afraid of disappointing others: friends, parents, teachers, Ms. Lungren, even the clerk at the grocery store.

When I pick apples from the produce bin, I rearrange the ones left in the display so there are no holes." A paint chip wedges under her nail, and she winces. "Pretty creepy, huh?"

"No, it's just you being . . . being you."

She toes the bits of brown dusting the floor. "And sometimes being me may not be a great thing." She tries to smile, but it comes across as a twisted grimace.

"Never apologize for being you." That's what my mom used to say.

"Really?" Kennedy looks up at me with eyes that care way too much about what I say.

"You know what?" I add. "This entire conversation is creepy, and it needs to end."

Kennedy shakes the paint chips from her fingers, her ponytail once again bobbing. "Not before I thank you for being here for me. People are exactly where they need to be when they need to be there. You were here for me when I needed you, and I'm here for you." Her hand settles over mine. "Remember that. It's fate."

I stare at our hands, speechless.

Footsteps clatter in the hall, and I spin toward the door. *Please, please, let it be Lungren or anyone to shut up Ms. What-Color-Is-Your-Heaven.* Nope. It's Percy, the head custodian. He rolls in with his cleaning cart and checks the underside of a desk in the back row. He takes a shiny spatula from his belt and scrapes off a wad of pink. After checking all the desks, he wipes the whiteboard, empties the wastebasket, salutes me with the gum scraper, and walks out, his left eye twitching.

Kennedy clucks her tongue. "Case in point, Percy Cole."

I bang my forehead on the desk. "You're not going to shut up, are you?"

"Haven't you heard his story?"

"I hate stories," I say to the desktop.

"Well, you're going to love this one. Percy served in Desert Storm and was on a supply mission when a roadside bomb went off. Eleven soldiers, including the men on either side of Percy, died. Why? Why did he live? It's destiny, I say. A force bigger than all of us kept him here, and he's alive because he's still needed here."

My head snaps upright. "To scrape gum off desks?"

"Only the fates know."

"The fates know squat. I control my own destiny."

"To some degree, yes. We have power over how we respond to events and our attitude about them, but I passionately believe there's a higher being or unseen force that places us where we need to be when we need to be there. I think you and I, Rebel Blue and Kennedy Green, are meant to be right here in this room right at this moment talking about this subject. Blue and Green. We're linked. Destined to share each other's journeys."

"I think Lungren was having a PMS kind of morning." I cover my face with my notebook.

"You're pushing me away again," she says with something that sounds like amused wisdom. "But that's okay. You have a guarded heart. The glowering looks, the snarky comebacks, even the shark teeth on your bag—they're all designed to keep people away. But we all need friends, and I consider you a friend."

I lower the notebook. "We are *not* friends! We're two strangers stuck in detention. I don't care about your fears. I don't care about the fates. For all I care, you and your turtles can take a one-way trip to your golden heaven."

Her lips form an O, and she turns stiffly in her chair. I jab my pencil into my notebook and scribble all the things I want to do before my butt lands in a casket and starts to decay.

"Hey, it looks like you got into it, too." Kennedy stands over my desk, grinning. "Wasn't this whole bucket-list thing fun?"

I squint at my notebook and blink. The page is full of words.

"It's five o'clock, and Ms. Lungren isn't back," Kennedy says. "I wonder what happened to Macey. She looked upset." She tugs at the end of her ponytail. "We should probably help her. You know, find her and let her know detention isn't the end of the world, that this whole bucket-list thing was fun."

I study the words bleeding across the page, words supposedly mined from the deepest part of my heart. A sharp, unexpected ache fills my chest.

"What are we supposed to do with our lists? We can leave

them on the desk for Ms. Lungren." Kennedy taps her chin with her pen. "But she told us to keep them. Maybe we should make copies. Then we can take the notebooks with us."

My finger slides over the final two lines, little more than faint scratches. The page blurs.

A hand lands on my arm. "Rebel, did you hear me? Maybe we should make copies."

I tear the list from the notebook and wad it into a ball. Tighter. Smaller. Impossible to read. I lob the paper into the trash. This assignment, the entire idea of digging deep into my heart, is a waste of my life. "Maybe we shouldn't."

Kennedy's mouth puckers in surprise, and a second later a tiny grin sneaks onto her lips. "Yeah, maybe we shouldn't." She casts a nervous glance at the doorway and then tosses her list into the trash.

I sling my messenger bag across my chest and rush out of the detention room. Away from Kennedy. Away from that list.

Kennedy follows, her ponytail no longer bobbing but bouncing. "I think you're an interesting person. And fun."

The gate at Unit Eight is locked. I race-walk down the breezeway and try the gate near Unit Four. Also locked.

"Maybe we can go out for chai tea sometime and talk. People say I'm easy to talk to."

I try the gate near the gym. No go.

"Or smoothies. Would you like to go out for smoothies?"

"I'd rather drink a cup of kitty." I mentally blot out annoying inspirational posters of kitties in teacups and sprint through the quad, the ache in my chest growing. Stupid cigarettes. Finally I reach the main gate and freedom, but I don't celebrate. Aunt Evelyn is going to explode when she hears about detention, a blowup of nuclear proportions.

Kennedy pops up beside me and rests her hand on my shoulder. "You don't look well. Do you need something?"

I slide my fingers along my messenger bag, the shark teeth strung across the strap making a comforting tinkle. "I need a bomb shelter."

Goodbye, Rebel Blue

1. Jump into a taxi and scream, "Follow that car!"

CHAPTER
TWO

AFTER DETENTION, I WALK INTO THE HOUSE AND toss my messenger bag at one of the brass hooks near the kitchen door. The bag slams into the wall and crashes to the floor. I wait for the shriek, *Rebecca, pick that up!*

But the house is silent.

Strange, because Aunt Evelyn lives by the motto *A place for everything, and everything in its place.* She's a residential stager, which is a type of interior designer. Before people put their houses up for sale, they hire the Aunt Evelyns of this world to redecorate, rearrange, and revitalize their homes in order to lure in the highest, fastest bids. Our home, a two-bedroom, Craftsman-style bungalow, is her picture-perfect portfolio.

I grab an apple from the ceramic rooster on the kitchen table and head down the hall to the bedroom I share with Penelope. Cousin Pen sits at the desk on her side of the room. She's thumbing through her calc book and humming. People who hum while doing math are perverted.

Penelope is the type who *gets* math. And cupcakes. On her fifteenth birthday last year, Penelope received cupcakes from her "bestest" buds, all seventeen of them. Since we share a bedroom, I lived with crumbs and the disgusting smell of buttercream frosting for a week. At the beginning of week two, I tossed the remaining cupcakes over the back fence for Tiberius, the next-door neighbor's rat terrier who has a sweet tooth and serious dental issues.

I kick off my flip-flops, and they soar across my side of the room, where they crash into a pile of laundry. "Where's your mom?" I ask Pen.

"At school." *Hummmmmm.* "She's meeting with the dean of students and your math teacher."

I dig through the rumpled sheets on my bed and find my sketchbook. "Now there's a double shot of happy."

"Not for you." Her humming sounds like a chain saw.

I tuck the sketchbook under my arm and bring the apple to my mouth but don't bite. "Say it."

"Say what?"

"Something that will no doubt bring me great pain and misery."

Pen looks up from her calculus. "Mom's really pissed. Because of detention this afternoon, you missed the math tutoring session she scheduled with Mr. Hogan."

"Bummer. I so love math." I take a bite of apple and, before she starts humming again, escape down the hall.

At the back of the Craftsman-style bungalow there's a tiny laundry room, and in the ceiling is a drop-down door. Uncle Bob calls the room above this door the attic crawl space. Aunt Evelyn calls it a storage area. I call it heaven.

I reach for the frosted piece of amber sea glass hanging from a string on the door, when the staccato clip of high-heeled shoes sounds behind me, followed by the sharp words, "Give me your scooter key. Now!"

Aunt Evelyn stands in the laundry room doorway. A single vein thickens and reddens in her neck.

The tumbled glass digs deeper into my palm. "Why do you need my key?"

"While you were in detention, I talked with school administrators and a few of your teachers, and things don't look good. You're a smart girl, Rebecca, and capable of doing A work. Look at your grades in AP English. Your abysmal grades in math and biology clearly show you're not studying enough, so I'm taking away your scooter for the rest of the week. No scooter means no long after-school bike rides, so you'll have more time to study."

I slap my palm on my forehead. "Oh, I get it now. It makes

so much sense. Would you also like my right kidney and first-born?"

"Rebecca, stop being a smart-ass!" A hissing spray of spit shoots from my aunt's lips, iced with coral lipstick that perfectly matches her pumps and sweater set.

"Would you like me to be a dumb-ass?"

Aunt Evelyn's lips pinch so hard, the lipstick rises in snaky ridges. I'm failing math, but I'm extraordinarily good at pushing buttons. She slicks her tongue over her lips and smooths the ridges. "All I want, Rebecca, is for you to study more."

I steady my hand on a giant rack of cleaning products. Across the rack is a string of paper cranes Cousin Pen made last year in support of nuclear disarmament. "Grounding me for the rest of the school year and locking me in a room with only my algebra book for company won't help. I don't get Algebra II. I already talked to my math teacher. The goal is to get through class this year with a D, and right now, that's doable."

"Ds are unacceptable in this household. You need to study more. Penelope studies four hours a day and gets straight As."

But I don't live on the same planet as practically perfect Cousin Penelope. We don't even breathe the same air. "Study? You want to talk about studying? Fine. I studied all week for that math test, including three hours the night before. I spent my entire lunch hour going over the test review sheet. I tried. Do you hear me? I. Tried."

"Try harder."

"You don't get it, do you?"

"Get what?"

"The rules. I don't get the stupid rules!" I bang a fist on the cleaning rack. Paper cranes sway, and a bottle of cleanser crashes to the ground. Blue liquid leaks onto the floor. The humming down the hall stops.

Even here in the laundry room, my head spins with the jumble and tumble of all those math-y rules. One of my tutors in junior high explained that math is a series of building blocks with clear and constant rules that determine the placement of those blocks. My problem: a faulty foundation. My mom homeschooled me until age ten, and she wasn't big on math. Or rules. Until I moved to Tierra del Rey, I did most of my studies curled up in the back of our ancient Jeep as we puttered across the Americas while Mom shot photographs. I studied history at Mayan ruins and biology in the Amazon rain forest. My English texts were dog-eared classics Mom dug up at used bookstores. And art, the study of light and color and shapes, was everywhere. All this left little time for math.

Aunt Evelyn picks up the bottle of cleanser. "Which is why you need to study more and attend the tutoring sessions I set up." She grabs a towel and wipes up the puddle of blue before setting her lips in a pinched smile. "I'll also get Penelope to review your homework and your teacher to send weekly updates and . . ."

She continues, but I block her out. Just like with math, I

tried. I tried to reason with my aunt, but you can't communicate with a person who doesn't speak the same language. I'll have to wait for Uncle Bob to get home. Uncle Bob is my mom's older brother. He's an accountant, a math guy, and while he doesn't always understand me, he isn't always trying to change me into something I'm not and never want to be.

When Aunt Evelyn finally stops lecturing, I pull the amber sea glass, and a door with a ladder unfolds. Once upstairs, I throw open the dormer windows. Lances of sunlight stream across the attic and strike the jars of sea glass crowded onto shelves on the back wall, sending colorful bits of light tumbling like confetti through the room. Slivers of amber and yellow, wedges of blue, and dots of green dance on the attic walls. If I believed in Kennedy Green's "heaven," it would be the color of confetti light.

I sink onto my chair and plug in my soldering iron. I run my fingertips along the wooden picture frame I whitewashed yesterday and a jar of sea glass the color of splintered ice.

I found my first piece of sea glass the week I came to live with Uncle Bob and Aunt Evelyn, the week I buried my mother. I needed to escape all the people patting my hand and telling me my mother was in a better place, so I ran to the beach looking for shark teeth. With Mom I traveled the back roads and beaches of Mexico and Central and South America, where we chased light. Mom was a photographer, and her heaven, if she believed in one, would be full of evocative light.

Together Mom and I collected shark teeth, mostly in our travels around the Gulf of Mexico. In her unique take on a homeschool science lesson, Mom explained that sharks continually shed their teeth, which fall to the ocean floor, where they become fossilized points of shiny ebony, topaz, and pearl. "Jewels of the sea," Mom called them. For one of my science projects, I strung together a set of shark teeth and presented her with a necklace.

"How unique!" Mom exclaimed. "How extraordinary!"

In the sands of Tierra del Rey, I found no shark teeth, but I discovered frosted bits of glass, each tumbled smooth and dulled by years of sand and salty waves. In that first year after Mom's death, I collected enough glass to fill six Mason jars.

I dig my fingers into the jar, scooping out a handful of time-softened glass. Time to forget about Aunt Evelyn and Penelope and annoying girls who talk about death and destiny. Time to make something extraordinary.

"Good morning, class. I'd like you to meet Herman, a four-foot black-tipped reef shark in serious need of therapy." Mr. Phillips aims his pointer at a screen with an image of a one-eyed shark with half a dorsal fin, nine broken teeth, and a scar on his belly shaped like Baja California. I notice these details because I sit at the lab table in the front row, center, a not-so-brilliant idea concocted by Aunt Evelyn and Mr. Phillips during their last parent-teacher love-in. Both figured moving me to the front row would help me stay on task and be less disruptive.

"Looks like ol' Herman also needs a dentist," I say.

Mr. Phillips must have had an extra spoonful of sugar on his bran flakes this morning. He points to the screen. "For three years Herman lived in a ten-foot aquarium in the back room of some shady San Diego fish dealer. He spent every hour of every day in that cramped space until animal-rights activists found him a cushy new home in an Olympic pool–size habitat. With all that room to swim, you'd think Herman would be in sharky Shangri-la, but he stayed in a ten-foot space until the day he died."

"Doesn't sound like the brightest fish in the tank," I say, but none of my classmates laugh. They are too busy talking among themselves in hush-hush voices. And today I need a laugh. When Uncle Bob got home last night, a monstrous family battle broke out and ended with Aunt Evelyn slamming doors, Cousin Pen locking me out of our bedroom, and Uncle Bob ultimately allowing me to keep my scooter key.

Mr. Phillips waves his pointer. "Focus, class. We're starting a new unit on animal behaviors, and we'll learn more about the Hermans of this world and why they do what they do."

"I'm trembling with excitement," I say. I'm only snarky in biology and sometimes Algebra II. Frustration fuels my math outbursts. My war with Mr. Phillips is rooted in all things Penelope. My cousin is a science rock star. I can't carry a tune.

Mr. Phillips stares at the ceiling. *To give detention, or not to give detention: that is the question.* In my defense, I'm the only one paying attention to his lecture on Herman the shark. The classroom buzz gets louder. Somewhere in the back of the room, someone sniffles.

At the lab table across from mine, a football type with a short, thick neck nudges another guy of the jockish persuasion. "Did you hear about the accident?"

"Yeah," Jock Number Two says. He wears a light blue preppy shirt and pressed khakis and has a scrubbed, squeaky-clean look. "Kennedy Green." He shakes his head, but not a single hair moves. "Wow."

I spin my pencil between my thumb and forefinger and wonder what's up with Kennedy What-Color-Is-Your-Heaven Green.

"It's horrible," No-Neck Jock says.

"I can't believe it," Mr. Squeaky Clean adds. "I can't believe she's dead."

My pencil clatters to the desk. I must have heard wrong. I tap Mr. Squeaky Clean on the shoulder. "You're not talking about Kennedy Green, are you? The girl with the . . . uh . . . blond ponytail?"

"Ms. Blue, you seem uncharacteristically social this morning," Mr. Phillips says. "Is there something you need to share with the entire class?"

I don't turn from Mr. Squeaky Clean.

"Were you her friend?" he asks.

You are a moron. "Casual acquaintance."

"She died last night. Her car slammed through a guardrail at Diego Point and crashed into the sea below."

The skin at the back of my neck prickles. Less than twenty-four hours ago, Kennedy and I talked about death and gold ladies and heaven. Strange coincidence.

It's fate.

I snort so loudly, Mr. Phillips taps my desk with his pointer. Mr. Squeaky Clean frowns, and in my head, Kennedy continues to jabber. *I passionately believe there's a higher being or unseen force that places us where we need to be when we need to be there.*

I pick up the pencil and spin it some more. *Well, Kennedy, you must have pissed off said higher being or unseen force.* The pencil clatters to the desk again. More than once Mr. Squeaky Clean glances at me. Not that he's looking at me in *that* way. He gives me the look he might give Herman the mentally disturbed shark.

During the rest of class I refrain from smart-ass comments and focus on Herman the shark, on Mr. Phillips's ugly tie—which today looks like a windshield after a cross-country road trip—on anything but Kennedy Green's death, which in theory should be easy, as, until yesterday, I'd never spoken to Kennedy Green. For two hours we sat in detention together, a far-from-memorable blink in a lifetime of fluttering eyelashes.

With five minutes left of class, the intercom beeps. "Mr. Phillips, can you please send Rebecca Blue and Nate Bolivar to the office?"

I want to kiss the little speaker box above Mr. Phillips's desk. Finally, something normal in my world. Mr. Squeaky Clean, who must be Nate, does not share my joy at being called to the office. He stands, his forehead scrunched. He's not the delinquent type, like Kennedy Green.

Dead Kennedy Green.

A police officer with a shiny badge and shinier bald head meets Nate and me in a small conference room in the school guidance center. "Good morning, Rebecca, Nate."

I sit on the edge of the chair nearest the door and wrap my arms across my chest. The cold, hard shark teeth on my messenger bag bite into my bare arm.

The officer pulls out a tablet. "I'm not sure if you heard yet, but one of your classmates, Kennedy Green, died in a car crash last night. We're investigating, and, as we understand it, you were two of the last people to see her alive."

My flip-flops shuffle under my chair. Kennedy was right; I'm not the sort who likes talking about death. I'd rather talk about sharks with psych issues.

The officer taps on his tablet. "We need to know Kennedy's mind-set yesterday afternoon. Was she happy, sad, upset? Did she seem nervous or agitated?"

"Why?" I ask. Keep him talking. That way I don't have to talk about death. After Mom died, Aunt Evelyn desperately wanted to talk about my *feelings*. "It's okay to be sad," she kept insisting. "It's normal to cry, Rebecca. You can cry. Why aren't you crying?"

The officer clears his throat. "The car crash that killed your friend was a single-car incident, and we're investigating to determine if it was accidental or purposeful."

I scrape my jaw from the floor. "Suicide? You think Kennedy Green committed suicide? She was the world's happiest person." People who plan on decorating the gym for prom next month don't kill themselves.

"There were no adverse weather conditions, no road hazards, and that portion of the highway is straight," the officer explains. "We need to determine her state of mind at the time, and you two should be best able to tell us."

Early in detention, Kennedy sobbed a river of snot and tears and was beating herself up for getting detention, but I calmed her and . . .

My blood chills.

. . . and told her and the endangered sea turtles to go to their golden heaven.

"So, Rebecca, was Kennedy distraught, or did she act in any way strange when you two were in detention?"

I lose my ability to speak. Kennedy was upset, but was she upset enough to kill herself? Did my snarky comments and less-than-warm-and-fuzzy behavior send her over the edge?

Of course they didn't. We were strangers, two girls sharing two hours of despised detention. I don't have a big enough ego to believe I have that much power over someone. Plus there's the fact that Kennedy left detention chipper and cheery. She invited me to go out for smoothies.

I'd rather drink a cup of kitty.

The room grows colder, darker.

Nate clears his throat. "Kennedy was fine at the 100 Club meeting, excited about getting the bird habitat we've been working on done. But she was late. That was strange because Kennedy is—was—always on time."

"She had detention," I say. "We were both in detention for doing something"—the entire room brightens as if a giant lightbulb bursts to life—"'dangerous, even deadly,' Ms. Lungren said. Maybe Ms. Lungren caught her doing something to harm herself. I don't know what she did to end up in detention. She never said." And I never asked. Because I wanted her dead, but not *dead* dead.

"Yes, I talked to Ms. Lungren already," the officer says. "She explained that Kennedy was in detention because she'd driven recklessly into the school parking lot yesterday morning."

Nate nods. "She sped out of the parking lot after the club meeting really fast, too. Tires squealing."

I sink back in my seat. "She said it was a crazy-busy day, and she was probably driving crazy."

The officer types notes on his tablet. "Yes, sounds like Kennedy wasn't the safest of drivers yesterday, but in the interest of leaving no stone unturned, did anything happen at the club meeting or detention to upset her?"

Nate shakes his head.

I try to shake off the image of me calling her a moron, which was said in a flash of irritation, not even anger. I was irritated that I had to write a stupid bucket list and worried about Aunt Evelyn's reaction.

After a moment or two of silence, the officer motions for us to stand. "Thank you, and I'm sorry about your friend."

We are not friends!

Let's not forget that nugget, either.

Outside the office, the halls are empty and silent except for the echo of our footsteps. Second period must have already begun, which is good because I need quiet. I gnaw the inside of my cheek and think. At the beginning of detention, Kennedy had been emotionally and physically distraught—enough for even me to notice.

Nate takes a step toward me, reaching out but not touching. "You okay?"

I give him my back-away-from-the-bubble look.

"Whatever." He glances at his watch and hitches his backpack onto his shoulder. "We'd better get to class, or we'll get detention."

Detention! Of course. I need to get to the detention room to find Kennedy's bucket list. Her list will shed light on her emotional and mental state, and because Percy emptied the wastebasket before we left, the crumpled piece of paper still sits in it.

I run to Unit Seven, but the detention room is locked. I run outside. The Del Rey School has long, one-story buildings with thick adobe walls and narrow windows designed to keep out heat. In late spring, most of the windows are cracked open. Pressing myself against the side of the building, I hurry to the third window. At five feet tall, I'm too short to reach. I jump, my fingertips clawing the ledge.

"Breaking and entering is illegal."

My fingers slip, but I dig my nails into the adobe again. "You scared the crap out of me," I say to Nate, keeping my voice low. I haul myself up to the ledge, where I anchor my elbows, reach inside, and tug on the window crank. It groans and creaks open. I crank faster. The handle snaps off. "Damn!"

"Defacing school property is also illegal," Nate says in a loud voice.

I toss the crank to the ground, and it lands wonderfully close to his right tennis shoe. "If you're going to narc, do it already, and shorten this special moment."

He crosses his arms. "Exactly what are you doing?"

"Breaking and entering," I say.

"Why?"

"I love detention." I wrench open the window, pitch my body through the narrow space, and crash into a stack of chairs. The chairs scatter across the room, and I scramble to my knees and listen. A door opens somewhere at the end of the hall.

Bolting to the wastebasket, I grope until I find two wadded-up pieces of paper, one covered mostly in doodles, the other, twenty neat lines.

"What's that?"

"Shit!"

Nate stands six inches behind me, his fists on his hips, his biceps straining against the sleeves of his polo, like some preppy detention-room guardian. He crawled through the window without a sound, all strength and agility and grace. Definitely a sporto.

He tilts his chin at Kennedy's bucket list in my shaking hand. "What's that?" he asks again.

I jam the paper into the thigh pocket of my cargo pants. "Trash."

"Now you're stealing."

"Someone threw it away. How can that be stealing?"

"It's not yours."

"It's trash!"

Footsteps clomp outside in the hallway. The door handle rattles. No time to argue about garbage. I stuff the other list into my pocket, rush to the window, grab a chair, and balance it on a desk. Climbing my makeshift ladder, I hurl my body through the window and don't bother to worry about how Mr. Squeaky Clean is going to get out of this mess.

2. Go for a job interview at
The Pork Shop and answer all the
questions in pig Latin

CHAPTER
THREE

THE LUNCH BELL RINGS, BUT I DON'T HEAD FOR MY
normal spot near the bike racks, a lunchtime hangout haunted
by the Del Rey School's other detention regulars. Nor do I go
to Miss Chang's fifth-period art class, where I sometimes help
her first-year students. I would never set foot in the cafeteria, a place for people wanting to see and be seen, like Cousin
Penelope and the Cupcakes. Instead, I swim upstream through
the crush of bodies to the locker courtyard in search of Death.

At a locker bay near the drinking fountains, I spot a black
hoodie. "I need to show you something," I tell Macey.

Macey throws her math book into her locker and pulls out
two bulging plastic grocery bags. "What?"

I slip my hand into my pants pocket, my knuckles brushing the piece of paper I'd stolen from the detention-room wastebasket. After checking into second-period AP English, a class I actually enjoy, I got a pass and spent most of the hour in the bathroom near the auto shop building reading Kennedy Green's bucket list. "Not here. It's something kind of personal."

Macey closes her locker. "I'm . . . uh . . . kind of busy."

I take one of Macey's bags and tilt my head at the end of the locker bay. "Fine. We'll talk while you do your 'busy.'"

For a moment, Macey looks startled, but she takes me along the breezeway to Unit Four and into one of the Family and Consumer Science classrooms.

The FACS teacher waves at us. "Hi there, Macey. I'm so glad you decided to come after all. And you brought a friend! Wonderful. The kitchen's ready. Let me know if you girls need any help."

Macey mumbles something that sounds like *I'll be fine* or *You have the eyes of a swine*. She takes her bags to one of six tiny U-shaped kitchens and unloads a truckload of strawberries and bags of sugar and flour.

I hoist myself onto the counter, the heels of my flip-flops tapping a cupboard door. "Did you hear about Kennedy Green?"

Macey takes a large glass bowl and measuring cup from the cupboard. She opens a bag of flour and starts spooning flour into the measuring cup.

"She's the princess who was in detention with us yesterday. Blond ponytail." Perky no longer. I hop off the counter.

Macey puts the cup on a scale, squints, and scoops another spoonful of flour.

"She's dead."

Macey's spoon hovers above the measuring cup.

"She was driving home from one of her do-gooder meetings last night and had a car accident. She drove off a cliff." Images and sounds careen through my head. Rushing sky, tumbling rocks, a single scream. My breath quickens.

"Uh, excuse me."

My eyes pop open.

Macey points at the cupboard behind me. "I need salt." She measures the salt and adds it to her bowl. "What does her death have to do with you?"

"Kennedy's death has nothing to do with me." *Blue and Green. We're linked. Destined to share each other's journeys.* I start to pace around the tiny kitchen, my flip-flops slapping the bottoms of my feet.

Macey takes a block of butter from a teeny-tiny fridge and slices and dices it into a million pieces.

"Would you stop the Martha Stewart bit and read this?" I wave Kennedy's bucket list in Macey's face. "Is there anything on here that makes you think she was suicidal?"

For the first time since we arrived in the FACS kitchen, Macey stills. She wipes her flour-dusted hands on the towel at her waist and takes the list, her pale, skeletal fingers careful, almost reverent. She studies the words. After a few minutes, she hands me the paper. "No."

A relieved breath whooshes from my chest. After reading the list, I didn't sense any suicidal or even angsty vibe, but I'm no psychology expert. Macey's second opinion reinforces my own that Kennedy's death was not suicide, and therefore I can put the entire thing out of my mind. I waltz to the trash can at the end of the row of kitchens.

"Stop!" An uncharacteristic pink flushes Macey's normally ghost-y cheeks. "You're not going to throw that away, are you?"

"It's a piece of paper."

Macey picks at a glob of buttery flour on the ragged cuff of her hoodie. "It seems weird to throw someone's . . . uh . . . dreams and desires into the garbage."

"What am I supposed to do with it? Have some sacred sending-off ceremony? Frame it and give it to her next of kin? Kennedy is dead. Dead people don't care about things left on Earth." I hold my hand over the garbage, where inside something with a brown body, long antennas, and grotesquely jointed legs skitters.

"Oh, no!" Macey cries.

I spin toward Macey. She wrings her hands as she stands over her mixing bowl. "I added too much water." She carries the bowl to the trash can, where she dumps the gray, gloppy mess onto the cockroach. A putrid odor, like sushi left in a locker over spring break, wafts from the garbage can. I turn away before I throw up, jamming the list into my pocket.

Back in her kitchen, Macey pulls out a new bowl and the measuring cup. A non-Macey-like light flares in her eyes.

"Exactly what are you doing?" I wonder how much stranger this day is going to get.

"Making a strawberry pie."

I rub at my forehead, where I imagine a thousand tiny cockroach feet skittering and scampering. "Why, Macey, are you making a strawberry pie?"

Her mouth turns down at the corners. "I couldn't find any peaches."

I consider ditching my afternoon classes, but that would lead to another stint in detention, which would detonate Aunt Evelyn, so I wait until the final bell to head to the beach. On the half-mile walk to the Pacific Ocean, seagulls screech overhead, and cars full of hooting and screaming students rush by me, but not loud enough to drown out the voice in my head.

I thought it would be kind of neat if we could be friends . . . Blue and Green . . . we're linked . . . maybe we can go out for chai tea sometime and talk . . .

Once at the beach, I kick off my flip-flops and dig my toes into the silky sand. Warmth creeps up my legs, across my chest, and along my neck, loosening the knots. I stroll along the water's edge. Despite the craziness of the day, or perhaps because of it, I hunt for sea glass.

Within minutes, I spy a clear wedge peeking from a crescent of gravelly sand. Clear glass is common, but I like the shape of this one. I slip the glass teardrop into my cargo pants pocket, the one that does not contain Kennedy Green's dreams and desires.

Unbuttoning the other pocket, I take out the paper. Time to ditch Kennedy's bucket list, and not in a malodorous, cockroach-infested garbage can with Macey giving me the stink eye. I shall give Kennedy's list wings. Literally.

I fold the paper in half and make a few diagonal creases in an attempt to approximate one of Cousin Pen's paper cranes. If I squint, I see a three-legged dog. Close enough.

With my arm raised toward the heavens, I fling the mutant canine. The wind catches the paper and whisks it higher. The girl who believed in a golden heaven would love this.

"Bye-bye, bucket list," I say with a jaunty wave. Good. Mission Get-the-Do-Gooder-Dead-Girl-out-of-My-Head accomplished.

My pocket and heart exponentially lighter, I jog three steps when something smacks me in the forehead and falls to the sand.

The bucket-list-mutant-crane-dog.

I jump back as if it might bite. Then I slap my palm on my forehead. Look who's wearing the I'm-a-Moron T-shirt now. I snatch the piece of paper, squeeze, and hurl it into the churning waters of the Pacific.

A kid wearing a beach towel like a Superman cape hops in front of me. "Hey, lady, that's littering." His face puckers in a scowl.

"It's paper. It'll dissolve."

"You littered. That's against the law. I'm going to tell my mom, and she's going to tell the lifeguard, and you're going to be in trouble."

I point to the sand toys a few yards up the beach. "Don't you have a sand castle to build?"

"You'll get a five-hundred-dollar fine and spend a hundred years in jail." He sticks out his tongue.

"Or maybe you should go stick your head in the sand."

His chubby fingers dig into the sides of his Superman cape, and his bottom lip juts out. "You're meeeeean."

I squat so we're eye level. "And you're eeeeevil."

His scowl morphs into a wicked grin. "And you're still a litterbug. Mooooom! I found another one. Can I tell the lifeguard? You got to do it last time. Please, can I, pleeeeease?" He runs to a granola-type woman farther up the beach, who starts walking to the lifeguard tower.

I wade into the water, scoop up the stupid paper, waggle it at Superbrat, and jam the sodden mess into my pocket.

The next morning I walk into the kitchen and listen to grumbling at the far end of the street followed by melodious beeping. This is the happy sound of a Tierra del Rey garbage truck. When

I got back from my run-in with Superbrat, I tossed Kennedy's bucket list into the recycling bin.

Reaching into the refrigerator, I pull out a piece of cheese-cake with blueberry sauce left over from last night's dinner and smile. A sweet start to a sweet day.

Aunt Evelyn, who stands at the sink, makes a sputtering sound, as if she's choking. "We don't eat *that* for breakfast," she says. "We've been over this countless times, Rebecca. Breakfast is the most important meal of the day. You must follow the food pyramid and be properly fueled."

Until I moved in with Uncle Bob's family, I'd never heard of the food pyramid and didn't know about breakfast *rules*. Breakfast with Mom could be white rice and black beans in Costa Rica or juicy plums plucked from a tree growing in the wilds of Chile.

Aunt Evelyn clucks her tongue and grabs the cheesecake from my hand. "Your breakfast is on the table." She points to a staged breakfast on a rooster place mat: yogurt parfait, whole-grain toast with kumquat marmalade, and fresh-squeezed orange juice.

Today is too good of a day to argue about the food pyramid. I grab the toast and slather on marmalade. The bucket list is gone, and my world has been set right.

The grumbling grows louder as the recycling truck rolls in front of our house. I raise my fingers, ready to wiggle a fond farewell, but the beeping, the sound that indicates the truck is lifting a recycling bin heavenward, never starts. I jump from the table and run to the front window in the living room in time to see the garbage truck lurch past the driveway. "It missed our bin."

Uncle Bob pokes his nose over the top of his newspaper. "Nope. I didn't put it out this morning. The bin isn't full. We'll have it emptied next week."

"Nooooo!" I race out the back door and grab the recycling bin from the side of the house. I haul it to the curb and run after the garbage truck, jerking the bin behind me. "Come back! You missed one. Come baaaaack!"

The truck lumbers around the corner and disappears.

I stand in the middle of the street, my hands trembling as they curl around the bin's handle. Maybe it's gone anyway. Maybe Kennedy was right and there's an unseen force that deliberately moves people and things around like pawns on the giant chessboard of life. And maybe that force knows I need this list out of my life.

I hold my breath.

I crack open the lid.

Wrinkled, dirty, and damp, Kennedy Green's dreams and desires are still here on Earth.

3. Drink absinthe in a Paris rathskeller

CHAPTER
FOUR

"YOU'RE LATE, MS. BLUE."

I throw my biology book onto my lab table.

"More than two minutes this time," Mr. Phillips continues. "Perhaps you should invest in a quality timepiece."

I toss my messenger bag under the lab stool. "I don't believe in quality timepieces." Nor do I believe in destiny or kismet or juju winds. I've never owned a rabbit's foot or good-luck Peruvian *huayruro* seeds. I don't avoid black cats and ladders. I chart my own course, control my own destiny.

So theoretically I should have no problems making the choice to get rid of Kennedy Green's bucket list. It's not something that requires the mastery of complex math functions. I need to toss the list into a garbage can, walk away, and forget about it.

I sink onto my stool. My flip-flops fall to the floor, and I wrap my toes around the lab-stool rung. I keep hearing Kennedy's annoying voice, keep reading her stupid list. Last night I dreamed Aunt Evelyn wallpapered a decorative border of Kennedy's list below the crown molding in my bedroom. I woke up sweating and shaking.

At the front of the room, Mr. Phillips taps his pointer on the podium. "Today we will continue our study on animal behaviors, and our topic this morning is pretty sexy."

Snickers roll through the classroom, and No-Neck Jock at the lab table next to me makes a crude comment about going animal with the girl behind him.

"Neanderthal," I say under my breath.

"Mutant," he mutters back.

The other jock, Nate of Great Hair, takes out a pencil and opens his notebook. I haven't seen him since he witnessed me heading off into the sunset with a dead girl's bucket list. I wonder if he got busted. I wonder if he's angry. I can't tell because he's ignoring me.

This morning Mr. Squeaky Clean is Mr. Squeaky Clean in a dark suit, white shirt, and blue striped tie. He looks good dressed up, but Nate Bolivar would look good dressed in a fig leaf. My gaze darts to the fetal pig on Mr. Phillips's desk. Not that Nate's my type. He follows rules and shines his shoes.

For the next half hour Mr. Phillips talks about the mating rituals of Adélie penguins. The big sexy: Instead of gifting their beloveds with diamonds, smitten male penguins drop rocks at their future mates' webbed toes. If the female penguins are feeling the love, they bop bellies and join in a mating song. If my mind wasn't so preoccupied with Kennedy Green's bucket list, I'm sure I could come up with a snarky comment that involves similar rituals at Del Rey School dances.

I tap my bare foot against the rung. Getting rid of the list shouldn't be this difficult. It means nothing to me. Kennedy means nothing to me, and I don't mean that in an unkind or spiteful way. Until detention, we had never spoken to each other. We had no common friends, no connections. So why can't I get rid of the list?

Only the fates know.

Shut up, Kennedy. I scrub my knuckles against my temples.

Nate lifts his head and glances at me out of the corner of his eye. He gives me a curious but slightly disgusted look, like most people give the fetal pig on Mr. Phillips's desk.

Don't mind me, Nate. I'm having a mental conversation with a dead girl. I pick up my pencil stub and jab it so hard against my notebook, the lead breaks.

Mr. Phillips gives us the last twenty minutes of the period to work on the lab packet for this month's animal behavior unit, something about ants. I dig a new pencil stub out of my bag. Next to me Nate whizzes through the first two pages and then closes the lab packet and centers it on his lab table.

"Nate, if you're done, why don't you give Rebel a hand?" Mr. Phillips shakes his head, and his glasses shift to the end of his nose. "She seems unable to get past question number one today."

My lab packet sits on my desk, the margins full of drawings of hundreds of ants, each carrying tiny bits of paper in its mouth.

Nate's jaw hardens as he scoots his lab stool next to mine. I brace my hands on my thighs. Now he'll tear into me for leaving him to take the blame for breaking into the detention room. I dig my index finger into a tiny hole in my cargo pants at a pocket seam. When I bolted, I had no intention of getting him into trouble. Self-preservation was the only thing on my mind. Plus, he chose to crawl through the window. I didn't drag him with me. I'm responsible for my own actions and he for his.

Staring at the clock on the wall, Nate is motionless except for one shiny dress shoe, which jiggles and squeaks on the rung of his lab stool. I can't tell if the shoe's too tight or if he's ready to explode. I pick up my pencil and spin it around my thumb. He tugs at the collar of his shirt.

"Well?" The word bursts out of my mouth against my will.

Nate blinks. "Excuse me?"

"Did you get busted for being in the detention room?"

"If you mean, did I get caught, yes, I did. Mrs. Pope from two doors down found me."

I concentrate on the spinning pencil. "Did you get detention?"

"No. I told her I saw the open window and was worried about someone vandalizing or stealing school property, so I crawled in to investigate."

"And she believed you?"

"Of course. It's the truth."

"And you *always* tell the truth?"

"Of course."

I snort so hard, I almost fall off my lab stool.

Nate smooths the cuffs of his shirt even though there's not a wrinkle in sight. "You don't know me."

The guy is making this way too easy. "True or false?" I ask. "When Mr. Phillips told you to help me, you didn't want to."

"What does that have to do with—"

"True or false?"

He lifts one shoulder in a dismissive shrug. "True. I don't want to do any more work right now because my mind's on other stuff, but I didn't lie to Mr. Phillips. I just didn't say anything."

"Exactly. You didn't state your truth."

"So you're saying people should *always* say whatever's on their minds. It doesn't matter if it won't change things or could hurt someone."

"People shouldn't be afraid to be themselves, which, yes, means stating their truths."

His lab stool stops squeaking as he leans toward me, every perfect hair staying in its perfect place. "So if you're all about truth, shouldn't you avoid things like breaking and entering, vandalizing, and stealing?"

I draw spiked hair on one of the ants. "That's *your* truth."

"Truth is truth, especially when we're talking about clear school rules."

"Whatev."

Nate snatches the pencil. "You don't want to argue because you know I'm right," he says with a confidence that would annoy me if I let myself be annoyed by people like him.

I snatch back the pencil. "I broke into the detention room because I had to do something that was important to me. I honored my truth."

He cocks his head. I draw another ant. Thanks to my blue streaks and the shark teeth, I'm used to people staring. The problem with Nate is, it's as if he's trying to stare past all that.

"So why the monkey suit?" I ask. "Trying to get a few extra votes for prom king?"

He glances at the clock. "Celebration of Life for Kennedy Green."

She's like a weed, popping up everywhere, and not just in my head. Yesterday during last period, the entire school had a moment of silence in her memory, and this morning someone lined the main breezeway with green balloons. "Celebration? Sounds like fun. Will there be an oompah band and bean dip?"

"Kennedy's parents are having the funeral in Minnesota where all the family is, but they decided before they leave tomorrow to have a celebration for their neighbors, co-workers, and friends." He digs into his pocket and takes out a small wooden turtle on a thong made of blue leather. No, *blue-green.* His finger slides along the turtle's sloped shell, and the hard set of his jaw relaxes. "She made this."

She. Kennedy. "You knew Kennedy well?" *Do you hear her voice? Have you formed an unhealthy attachment to items once in her possession?*

"I worked with her on quite a few service projects this year." Nate holds out the turtle necklace. "A few months ago Kennedy made one hundred of these and sold them to raise money for endangered sea turtles. In her excitement, she forgot to save one for herself. I told her I'd give her mine." He winds the cord around a finger. "But I never did." The cord wraps tighter about his knuckle, biting into flesh.

If I were the touchy-feely type, now would be the time to pat his arm. "Sucks to be you."

He lets go of the turtle, and the leather thong loosens. "I plan to give it to her mom and dad at the Celebration of Life. They should have it. It was important to her."

Like Kennedy's bucket list, which smolders in my pocket. For the rest of the period, I ignore the burning sensation and, with Nate's help, answer questions about ants.

Near the end of class, Nate stands and waves to Mr. Phillips.

A dozen more students stand and gather their backpacks. I try to ignore the words forming in the back of my throat. But I can't stop them any more than I can stop ocean waves from tumbling sea glass.

"Uh, Nate." I speak too softly. He won't hear.

"Yeah?"

"Where is it?" My voice is a whisper. He'll walk out the door.

"Where's what?"

"The celebration of Kennedy Green's life."

4. Ride a shopping cart down the candy aisle at Target screaming, "The British are coming! The British are coming!"

CHAPTER
FIVE

"WHAT ARE *YOU* DOING HERE?" COUSIN PENELOPE whisper-screams as I walk into the Hope Community Church behind Nate.

Whisper-screaming is a difficult task to master, one that requires great skill and the ability to balance rage and a polite smile that indicates *No, I'm not about to beat my dear cousin over the head with a* Glory and Praise *songbook.* She clutches my arm, her talons digging into my skin.

"Let go, Pen," I say in a nonwhisper. "Unless you want even more people gawking at us." Throngs of Kennedy Green's friends, neighbors, and people she most likely annoyed on a regular basis all congregate in the church lobby.

Pen pulls me into a nook lined on three sides with stained glass and releases her death grip on my arm. "You can't come in here looking like *that*."

"I look fine."

"Normal people don't wear tank tops, cargo pants, flip-flops, and a ratty bag covered in shark teeth to a memorial service. You look like a thrift-store reject."

When I dressed this morning, I had no intention of attending a Celebration of Life, but I need to get rid of Kennedy's bucket list. The side of my palm brushes against my pocket where Kennedy's final dreams and desires lie, all sure to spark joy and pride in any parental heart, because although she was annoying, Kennedy was a human being who cared about her family, her friends, and doing good. "Kennedy wouldn't care what I wore to her service."

"How would you know?" Pen asks with a snap. "You didn't even know her."

In life, I knew Kennedy for two hours, but I read her bucket list. I held a piece of her heart. She told me her fears, and she got me to admit mine. I knot my fingers behind my back. "Kennedy wouldn't care if a homeless person showed up in duct-taped shoes. She'd see the value of the person and the gift of that person's presence."

My cousin takes a step back as if I were doing a strange penguin mating dance.

No, I am not being my normal prickly self, because I cannot

be that self when I can't stop thinking about Kennedy's list, which means I need to get rid of said list so the world can get back to normal. I'm starting to dislike me. Pen doesn't argue, but she keeps a wary eye on me as the masses milling in the lobby, including many of her friends, file into the church.

"So how did you know Kennedy?" I ask. "She's not a Cupcake, is she?"

"Kennedy is—was—on the track team."

"I don't remember hearing about her."

Pen makes sure everyone knows about the accomplishments of the Del Rey School's championship women's track-and-field team, of which she is co-captain. "Kennedy didn't win any races, but she was important to the team, attending every practice, willing to help set up at meets, and helping the trainer." Sounds like Kennedy, a real team player.

Organ music swells inside the church. Nate, who's been waiting in the lobby with other jockish types, pokes his head into the nook and taps his watch. "We should get inside."

"Do not embarrass me." Pen spins on her Celebration-of-Life-appropriate brown leather flats and walks into the church. Nate follows, and they join a group of students in the center pews.

I slip inside and duck into the back row. The place is wall-to-wall people. My feet sweat. I'd never been to a Celebration of Life. I remember parts of Mom's service at Aunt Evelyn and Uncle Bob's church. Flowers. Black suits. Tuna casseroles.

Through the haze I remember tugging Aunt Evelyn's hand and whispering, "Mom hates tuna."

I also remember shoes with sparkly silver bows.

For my mom's funeral service, Aunt Evelyn bought me a blue dress with silver ribbon trim and navy shoes with silver bows. "Sparkly bows make everything better," Aunt Evelyn insisted. The glitter flaked off the bows and made my feet itch, and the pointy toes pinched. I took off the shoes just as an usher led us down the church aisle at the beginning of the service. Aunt Evelyn almost fainted.

No one faints at Kennedy Green's Celebration of Life, which is a series of inspirational songs, prayers, and speeches from the VIPs in Kennedy's life: favorite teachers, track coach, best friends, and fellow do-gooders. After the final song, I file in line behind Nate, who is behind Penelope, who hugs Mr. and Mrs. Green and goes on and on about how they were on the track team together and how much she admired Kennedy.

Sweat slicks my palms. *Hi, I'm Rebecca Blue, and I called your daughter a moron.*

Nate's next. I take notes. Firm handshake. Slight nod of head. Kind words. Calm voice. Respectful tone. Reach into pocket. Take out turtle. Give to Mrs. Green. Group hug.

Piece of cake. If you're Nate.

I wipe my palms on my pants. The person behind me nudges my back. I stumble forward. "Uh, hi."

Mrs. Green takes my hand in hers. Mr. Green nods.

"I . . . I went to school with Kennedy."

"Of course," Mrs. Green says. "She had so many friends at school, at church, and at all of the places where she volunteered. She was such a good girl and a good friend."

"She asked me out for chai tea."

"Kennedy loved chai tea. With vanilla and extra spice."

I nod, like one of those dolphins performing for a bucket of fish. Someone behind me clears his throat. "I have something of Kennedy's, something important, something she'd want you to have." I take out the list, wrinkled and dirty in the golden light streaming through the windows. I should have ironed it or steam-cleaned it or something. I pick off two bits of dried seaweed and flatten the paper against my thigh. Doesn't help. I throw it at Mrs. Green.

She catches the paper and reads. Tears well in her eyes. "A good girl. My Kennedy was a good girl who wanted to spend her life doing good things." Mrs. Green's chin trembles. "But you know what? I want you to keep this. If Kennedy gave it to you, you're someone dear to her."

I wave it off, but Mrs. Green presses the list onto my palm. I push back. She presses harder.

A sob wracks her body, and she shakes.

I shake.

Mr. Green wraps his arm around Mrs. Green's shoulders. "Maybe you should go," he says, looking at me.

Go? I can't move. The bucket list is a two-ton weight. Someone yanks my elbow. I'm led through stained light and hushed voices, past a collage of Kennedy with and without ponytails.

The list. I still have the list.

Once outside, Penelope releases my arm. "You made Mrs. Green cry!" She doesn't bother with the whisper part of her whisper-scream out here. "What did you do?"

"I tried to do something good." My voice is shaky. "I tried to give her something Kennedy wrote, something that was important to her, a list, her bucket list."

Nate points at the paper clenched in my fist. "This is what you stole from the wastebasket when you broke into the detention room, isn't it?"

I nod.

Penelope rubs the bridge of her nose. "You are so not related to me."

Nate makes a *hmm* sound. "Sounds like the type of thing a parent might want to keep."

I hold the list at arm's length as if it were covered in cockroach entrails. "But she didn't take it." I seize Nate's arm. He's Mr. Rock Solid. I'm a quivering mess, about to dissolve into a puddle. "Why didn't Mrs. Green take it?"

Penelope raises both hands in the universal sign language for *du-uh.* "Probably because her daughter died and this is the worst week of her life."

"Maybe she needs a little more time," Nate says. "I'd hang on to it for a while in case she asks for it."

I raise my fist and stare in horror at the possessed paper. "I can't throw this list away, because it won't let me throw it away."

Pen takes two steps away from me. "If you're going to have a psychotic episode, Reb, please don't do it in my presence."

"I'm serious." I proceed to spew. I spew about detention, bucket lists, destiny, chai tea, and police officers worried about suicide. I spew about the cockroach and shy, quiet Macey yelling at me, about the mutant paper crane dog and Superbrat. By the time I spew about the garbage man who drove past the house, I'm hoarse. "And now Mrs. Green insists I keep it. The list, I can't get rid of it. It's haunting me."

Nate stares at me oddly. Pen looks horrified. I don't need either of them. I spin, but Nate grabs my arm.

"Maybe Kennedy was right," he says. "Maybe it's a matter of destiny. Maybe you're meant to have that list."

"Why would I need Kennedy's bucket list?"

"So you can complete it."

"Stand back or risk me hurling all over your shiny shoes."

His face is serious. "Maybe there's something on there that needs to be done, and only you can do it. Maybe the fates chose you."

"Then the fates have knocked back one too many shots of tequila."

"Let me see." Penelope snatches the list. Her eyeballs dart back and forth as she reads every line. "I agree with Rebel."

Now there's a first. "See, Pen doesn't believe in this fate-destiny crap, either."

"I don't think it has anything to do with fate or destiny." Pen aims the list at my chest as if it were a dagger. "Kennedy Green was a good person who did a lot of good in this world. With this list, she planned on doing more good. She wanted to help people and make this world a better place. The issue, dear cousin, is that you're nothing like Kennedy Green." She jabs the list at my heart. "You're a wrecking ball." *Stab.* "You cause damage and destruction to everything you touch." *Stab.* "You hurt people and kill dreams." *Stab. Stab.* "You're incapable of doing good."

My heart pounds against the bag strap slung across my chest, urging me to run, but I can't move. Pen's blistering words melted my flip-flops, gluing them to the sidewalk. With a soft sob, Penelope drops the list and runs to a group of track-team members gathered in the parking lot. The paper floats through the air and lands on my left foot.

"You okay?" Nate asks. "Listen, funerals and deaths do crazy things to people. My Tia Mina laughed for two days when Tio Rogelio died, and two of my mom's second cousins got into a fistfight at their father's funeral. They knocked over the altar flowers, and the priest had to break it up. Funerals can bring out strong emotions in people. I'm sure Penelope didn't mean to sound so harsh."

I'm sure she did. Pretty Princess Penelope hated me from

the moment I moved into her house. That first week, she glared at me from across the dinner table when Uncle Bob helped me with my math homework. She threw a fit when Aunt Evelyn took me shoe shopping. She threw away my Mason jars of sea glass, and when I beheaded her Polly Pockets in retaliation, she declared war.

"You need a ride back to school?" Nate is concerned but calm and in control, like a guy you'd want on hand when the Big One strikes Southern California.

Unlike me. My entire upper body shakes, and the shark teeth on my bag rattle. My skin is hot. And sitting on my toes is that heinous piece of paper. I want to grind Kennedy's bucket list into the ground, to run after my cousin and scream at the top of my lungs that she knows nothing about me. Nothing.

You're incapable of doing good.

"No. I'm good," I tell Nate.

You hear that, Penelope? I. Am. Good.

Because as I've said all along, there's no such thing as fate or destiny. Life is one big choice after another. I can choose to do good for the entire world to see. I can choose to decorate the gym with toilet-paper flowers for prom. I can choose to save every stupid turtle in the sea.

I pick up Kennedy Green's bucket list and look into her heart.

MY BUCKET LIST
BY KENNEDY GREEN

1. Perform one random act of kindness every day for one year
2. Become a centurion for the Del Rey School 100 Club
3. Adopt an endangered leatherback turtle in each of my grandparents' names
4. Plant seedlings in Brazil to replenish our dwindling rain forests
5. Start my own 501(C)(3) charity
6. Learn American Sign Language and volunteer to sign for the hearing impaired at church
7. Spend the summer doing AIDS education in Africa
8. Go to Mexico and help build a home for a needy family
9. Donate my hair for cancer-victim wigs
10. Ride a bicycle built for two
11. Run a seven-minute mile
12. Participate in a flash mob
13. Sing in a living Christmas tree
14. Learn to tango
15. Host a tea party in a secret garden
16. Hike Mt. Everest with my brother
17. Make a complete Thanksgiving dinner from scratch for my family & friends

18. Make a time capsule with my family
19. Sleep on the beach with my best friend under the stars
20. Ride in a gondola in Venice, Italy, with the love of my life

"Are you sure you don't need a ride?" Nate asks.

I unfasten my cargo pants pocket and jam in Kennedy Green's bucket list. "I'm good," I say again. And I can choose to prove that Cousin Penelope is dead wrong.

5. Surf naked

CHAPTER
SIX

I POKE MY HEAD INTO THE BIOLOGY LAB. IT'S EMPTY, but then again, it's 6:30 A.M.

Throwing my messenger bag onto my lab table, I dig out the small paint scraper I found last night in one of Aunt Evelyn's decorator-supply tubs. Aunt Evelyn goes nuclear when anyone borrows her stuff without asking. Unfortunately for the fate of the Free World, I did not ask, as that would entail explaining Kennedy Green's bucket list, which is still in my possession although not because of destiny or juju winds. I'm hanging on to Kennedy Green's bucket list to prove that Cousin Pen is an idiot.

You're a wrecking ball. You cause damage and destruc-

tion to everything you touch. You hurt people and kill dreams. You're incapable of doing good.

I take great delight in being extraordinarily bad, but Cousin Pen is wrong. I can do good, and I can complete every item on Kennedy Green's bucket list, including the first: *Perform one random act of kindness every day for one year.*

Percy is my first victim.

I first met him my freshman year during a pep rally when he found me in the maintenance closet near the gym with my hands over my ears. The entire student body had gathered for a mandatory *rah-rah* session celebrating the football team's homecoming win. Since I'd been homeschooled and knew nothing about football fever, I wasn't prepared for shaking bleachers, blaring trumpets, and four thousand screaming classmates. After he found me hiding in the closet, Percy reached into a box on one of the shelves, took out a small plastic bag, and handed it to me. Inside, I discovered a pair of earplugs. "For when you need to turn off the world."

I still have the earplugs, because sometimes the world is still too loud.

The biology room is wonderfully silent as I search under the first stool and scrape off a bulbous pink glob with teeth marks. Stool number two is clean, as are three and four. At chair five I hit the mother lode, four wads, including a minty fresh one. After wishing the owner a root canal for his next birthday, I swipe the gum into my trash bag, but it clings to the scraper.

"Need some help?"

I jump, and the scraper falls onto my toe. "Will you stop sneaking up on me?"

"I didn't sneak," Nate says. "I called your name, but you didn't hear me."

"I was focused." I lift the scraper, and the gum hits my elbow.

"Let me help you"—Nate wrinkles his nose and then dispenses a crinkly paper towel from the wash station—"*un*focus."

"I don't need help." I shoo him away with the scraper, and a string of gum migrates to my hair.

"Sure you don't." Nate swipes at the gooey chain of gum that had traveled to my knee. Tucking in the paper towel as he goes, he tackles my flip-flop. Even bent over my foot, his wavy hair stays in place. "Did Mr. Phillips get tired of your snarky comments about his ugly ties?" Nate asks.

My right eyebrow shoots skyward.

"One of Lungren's detention assignments?"

Left eyebrow.

Nate's fast, efficient, and manages to get every speck of gum off me and the floor in the time it takes me to de-gum my hair. He wads the paper towel and lobs it into the trash can. Score another one for Nate the Great. He settles his butt against my lab table and stares.

"Don't you have hordes of other pretty people to go hang out with before school?" I throw away my gummy paper towel.

"I'm tutoring this morning." He stretches out his legs and

crosses his ankles. "This is about the bucket list, isn't it?"

I duck under the next lab stool.

"I'm impressed," he says grudgingly.

"Don't be. This has nothing to do with honoring the dead or being moved by destiny."

Nate continues to study me, as if I'm a wet bacterial culture under one of Mr. Phillips's microscopes. He's probably picturing me blubbering about possessed bucket lists or, worse, remembering Pen screaming. Pen can be annoying and mean, but I'd never seen her so angry, almost out of control. I wedge the scraper against the underside of the stool, and a wad of gum flies across the room, hits the fetal-pig jar, and rolls under Mr. Phillips's desk.

Nate reaches into his backpack and pulls out a notebook. "By the way, we'll meet today at my house at four."

I squat before Mr. Phillips's desk and search for the wad of gum. "I'm currently passing biology with a lovely C-minus, so I don't need tutoring."

"This isn't about tutoring but making the sea-swallow decoys."

"The what?" I grope under Mr. Phillips's desk, my palm sliding along crunchy, dusty things.

"The sea-swallow decoys, fake birds. Some of the club members will be painting them at my house after school today."

"Club?" The nail on my index finger digs into something squishy. Please let this be a wad of gum.

"You're rebelblue@ourworld.com, right?"

"Yeah. Are you some kind of stalker?"

"No. I'm the president of the Del Rey School 100 Club, and you e-mailed me last night wanting to know when our next meeting is. We're meeting at my house to paint bird decoys, which we'll set up on the beach later in the week. It's part of our community service project to protect and enhance the swallows' nesting grounds in Tierra del Rey."

Now everything makes sense, or as much sense as anything to do with Kennedy Green does. Item number two on her bucket list is *Become a centurion for the Del Rey School 100 Club*. According to the school website, the 100 Club is some kind of community service club, and I figured I'd need to pay dues and learn the secret "centurion" handshake. But apparently it also involves going to Nate's house and painting fake birds. "I'll have to check my calendar. You know how it is for us social butterflies. I might have, I don't know, a cotillion or something."

With half an eye roll, Nate scribbles on a notebook page and yanks out the piece of paper. "Here's my address."

Oh, goody, now I get to see where Nate keeps his hair gel. I cram the wad of gum into my trash bag and wonder if it's okay to swear at a dead girl.

"What's going on in here?" Mr. Phillips stands in the doorway, glaring at me sprawled beside his desk. "And what are you doing down there?"

I lift the bag of ABC gum. "I'm—"

"Stop!" Mr. Phillips takes a step back. "Put down the bag, Rebel."

"Hey, I'm—"

"And step away from my desk."

"What? You think this is a bomb or something?"

"Keep your hands out front where I can see them. No sudden movements."

Nate doesn't bother to hide a laugh.

"Dammit, I'm trying to do good!"

Two months ago, when I turned sixteen, Uncle Bob gave me a motor scooter that once belonged to my mom. Aunt Evelyn threw a fit. "Rebecca could get hurt," she insisted. "We can't afford the insurance. That thing is about to fall apart."

Uncle Bob is a pasty version of my mother. He has thin, light brown hair pulled over his head in a wispy comb-over, pale blue eyes, and the unassuming voice of a man who's content to live out his life as an accountant in a tiny cubicle, but when it came to Mom's Vespa, he wouldn't budge. "Reb has so little from her mother. She *will* have the scooter."

My mom bought the scooter secondhand three decades ago. Even back then it had an attitudinal starter and stalled at stoplights. I named the scooter Nova. Once Aunt Evelyn accepted the new two-wheeled family member, she reached into her little decorator heart and splurged on a paint job, celestial blue, and bought me a license plate holder with sparkly stars, suns, and comets.

"Quite fitting for a scooter called Nova, don't you think?" Aunt Evelyn asked with a clap of her hands.

At which point I informed her, "*No va* means 'no go' in Spanish."

More often than not, Nova sits in the garage refusing to scoot. Today is one of Nova's good days.

I love riding. I love the salty wind brushing my face, the blur of colors as I sail down a coastal hill, my legs stretched out, feet lifted. I love the idea that my mom rode this same bike through these same streets. Unfortunately, I'm not thrilled with my final destination: Nate's house.

As I putter away from the ocean, I leave the cottages and condos of the coastal hills and enter an older part of Tierra del Rey with run-down houses and weed-choked sidewalks. Somehow, I pictured Nate living in a seaside mansion. I have no problem with this part of town, but I figured a guy like Nate had it all, including money.

Nate's house sits at the end of a cul-de-sac. The tiny house has a tiny, neat yard. On the porch stands a sculpture of some holy guy with open arms. Before I get a chance to knock, the door swings open, revealing a girl, ten or so, with a long curtain of black hair and an ivory pillbox hat slung low on her forehead. She wears black leggings and a black sweater set adorned with a double string of pearls.

"I'm here to see Nate," I say.

She swishes back the gauzy veil of the hat and squints at me, as if she's looking into the sun or doesn't understand English.

"Nate?" I say louder, adding more slowly, "Is Nate here?"

"Beautiful," she says on a whoosh of air. Her breath smells sweet, like cherries.

"Excuse me?"

"Your hair. It's beautiful." She reaches for my head.

I duck. "Can you get Nate?"

"How did you get the streaks so blue?" She scrunches her nose and inches closer.

"Visit from the blue-hair fairy. Where's Nate?"

Another girl, this one older than the pillbox diva, joins us in the doorway. A violin dangles from her right hand. "Are you Nate's girlfriend?" She pushes her glasses to the bridge of her nose. "You don't look like the girls he normally brings home."

"Nope. Definitely not his girlfriend."

She taps the violin against her leg. "Do you want to be his girlfriend?"

"Hell, no!"

"You shouldn't swear," says another little person who appears in the doorway. This one's a boy, about kindergarten age. He wears underwear covered in dinosaurs.

"Why don't you want to be his girlfriend?" Violin Girl asks. "All girls who come over want to be Nate's girlfriend."

I take a deep breath and ask the pint-size trio, "Where's Nate?"

"Try the sunroom at the back of the house." This comes from a gray-haired woman in a red-sequin dress who struts across the entryway in red high heels.

I escape down a hall painted cheery yellow. Aunt Evelyn would call it something like Sunbeams in a Fondue Pot. In the kitchen I find a boy at the counter, a replica of Nate but three or four years younger.

"Oh, good," the kid says. "I'm glad you're here."

"I'm here to see Nate." I need a megaphone, a giant billboard, anything to get my message across to these people.

"First I need you to try my flan." Nate the Younger sticks a plate in my face. On it jiggles a flat, cream-colored pyramid oozing with shiny brown sauce. "I'm in charge of dinner tonight."

"I don't eat brown things that jiggle."

For a moment he looks heartbroken. Then he slaps his thigh. "Come back next week, and I'll make you flan with raspberry sauce."

Waving off the plate, I wander through a maze of more brightly colored rooms. At last I see a bunch of white plastic birds on a table in a sunny room overlooking the backyard. Another freaky religious statue, this one with angel wings and a large sword, stands in one corner.

I sit on the sofa far away from the saint and plop my messenger bag at my feet.

"Nooooo!" The plump, gray-haired woman with the slinky red dress wags her finger at me from a giant arched opening in the wall. "Purse! Get purse off floor. *Pronto!*"

I jerk my bag and feet off the floor. "Why? What?"

"If you keep purse on floor, all money walk off." She clucks her tongue as if I should know better and walks away.

I rub the center of my forehead where a tiny ache has settled. This house is strange and the people stranger.

Finally, Nate strolls into the room but comes to a stop when he sees me cowering on the sofa. "What are you doing?"

I unfold my body and pry my bag from my chest. "Desperately trying to keep my money from walking away."

"You must have met Tia Mina." Nate chuckles as he tosses a stack of newspapers onto the table. "She's a character."

"Are there any more *characters* with whom you share DNA that I need to be warned about?"

"Probably." He unfolds the newspaper and covers the table. "I have a big family."

"Including those little people." I don't hide a shudder.

"My brothers and sisters? I have to keep an eye on them once a week after school when Tia Mina goes to dance class and my parents are at work. Sometimes they can be a little annoying, but they're good kids."

Kids are not good. Aunt Evelyn signed up Pen and me for a course in babysitting when we were eleven. Pen got extraordinarily high marks while I failed everything but finger painting.

I think it's because I was never around other kids growing up.

I join Nate at the table and pick up a plastic bird, which looks like an anemic rubber chicken without feet. "So for this 100 Club, is there some type of paperwork I need to fill out to officially become a centurion?"

Nate distributes the birds around the table. "Technically, you can't be a centurion until you hit one hundred hours of community service for the year, but you can participate in activities and—"

"Wait." I aim the bird at his chest. "Are you telling me I need to spend one hundred hours painting ugly birds?"

"You need to spend one hundred hours doing some type of community service. We have about twenty more hours to get the nesting site ready for the sea swallows. We need to set up the decoys and fencing, prune back vegetation, and make the chick shelters."

I scratch my chin with the bird's beak. "And this is a hard-and-fast rule, this hundred-hour service requirement?"

"It's the *only* rule."

My fingers wrap around the bird's neck. I'm a girl who doesn't like rules, but Kennedy does. None of her bucket-list items are of the rule-breaking variety. Most of the items are about do-gooding, so by the time I finish them all, I'll probably be close to triple-digit goodness. I toss my bird onto the table. "Where's the paint?"

As I help Nate set up the paint and brushes, more members of the 100 Club arrive. Most perform a double take when Nate introduces me. Bronson, Nate's no-neck sporto friend from biology, squints at me, his face morphing from dumb jock to dumb, *confused* jock. "You realize this is a *service* club, right?"

"Oh, no!" I grab both cheeks. "I thought this was the quilting club."

The veins in Bronson's neck bulge. Nate steps between us, handing out photos of a bird with a black cap, gray and white body, and orange bill. "Here's what the swallows look like. Start painting."

Two girls, including one I recognize from AP English, plaster themselves on each side of Nate as he takes a spot at the head of the table. Mr. In Charge and Charming wears an easy grin as they chat about endangered birds and erosion of natural habitats. Bronson tosses his bird onto the table, knocking over a jar of gray paint that conveniently trickles my way.

I grab the paint before my bird drowns. "Watch it."

Bronson plops down on the couch and turns on a small television. "Sorry."

The puddle spreads toward the edge of the table. "Come clean this up."

"I'll supervise." He scrolls through the channels.

A boy next to me grabs a handful of paper towels and tosses them over the paint, but I wave him off. "Get your ass over here," I tell Bronson. "You made the mess."

"It was an accident." A baseball field appears on the TV screen, and he sets down the remote. "I'm all thumbs when it comes to artsy-fartsy stuff."

"I'm sure you have enough athletic prowess to wield a paper towel," I say. The chatter around the table stops.

"I said, I'll supervise." Bronson tucks a throw pillow under his head.

I drop my bird and step in front of the television. "And I said, clean up the mess."

"Why is it such a big deal to you?"

"Because the paint is all over my spot at the table."

"So why don't *you* clean it up?"

"Because I didn't spill it. I have no idea why we're even having this asinine conversation. You make a mess, you clean it up. Ever hear of personal responsibility?"

"Ever hear of Prozac?" Bronson asks. Giggles rise from all four sides of the table.

I jam my hands into my two back pockets. I'm on edge because I don't know how to deal with people like this, which is why I don't join clubs like this.

"Leave him be, Rebel," says the girl from AP English. "Seriously, he can't paint, so we don't want him anywhere near the table."

"Then why is he here?" I ask with raised palms.

"I need another thirteen hours before I hit a hundred," Bronson says.

"Wait. Let me make sure I understand this." I point both hands at Bronson. "You're earning service hours watching TV while we paint the birds."

"Sounds like a plan to me."

I spin toward Nate. "Isn't this in violation of the one club rule?" Not that I care about rules. The blatant-dishonesty thing is what boggles my brain.

Bronson crooks a finger at me, inviting me closer. "Here's a little secret a wallflower like you may not know. Nate will handle everything. He aces every class, every assignment, and he likes things done his way." He fluffs the pillow beneath his head. "He'd probably repaint my bird anyway. Isn't that right, Nate-O? No worries?"

We both turn to Nate, who is as still as the saintly statue in the corner. He stares at me as if I'm wearing underwear with dinosaurs. At last he walks across the room and switches off the TV. "Rebel's right. If you want the hours, you need to paint. Now let's get to work."

With Nate the Efficient at the helm, everyone in the room, including Bronson, starts painting. I pick up my paintbrush and study the jars of paint. Drama isn't my thing, and stuff like these power plays exhausts me. Art, on the other hand, is something I know and love. This gray paint is too dark for the feathers and not natural looking. I drop a dab onto my forearm and then add white and black until I get a nice, variegated gray. For community-service hours, there could be worse things than painting. I'll have to take a picture when I'm done and show it to Miss Chang, my art teacher. When I reach for my bird, I notice that everyone has stopped painting and is staring at me.

"What?" I ask.

The girl from English looks at me as if I have an orange beak sprouting from my forehead. "Most of us stopped painting ourselves in preschool."

"I'm mixing paint."

"Interesting . . . um . . . technique."

I dab my brush back into the paint on my arm. "Works for me." Sometime later, I go to dip my brush into the orange paint to finish the beak when Bronson grabs the jar. "I'm not done with it," I say.

"You've had it for five minutes," Bronson says.

"Ten," adds the girl from English. She taps her brush against her bird's unpainted beak.

"We can share. Bring your birds down here."

"They're wet."

"Okay, let me finish one thing." I aim my brush at the paint, and Bronson jerks it away. An arc of orange sails across the table and splats the face of the girl from English.

She swipes the orange from her eyes and mouth and stares in horror at her hands, as if she's dripping blood. "Look what you did!"

"I didn't do it. Bronson did."

"But it's your fault," she says.

"Like hell it is!"

Something tugs at my pocket. The littlest Bolivar, the one in the dinosaur underwear, frowns at me. "You shouldn't swear. You'll go to hell."

I'm already in hell.

6. Vacuum a magic carpet

CHAPTER
SEVEN

I SINK INTO THE CHAIR BEHIND MY DRAFTING TABLE and watch bits of confetti light tumble through the attic. After the ugliness at the 100 Club meeting, I'd love to grab my soldering iron and spend the late afternoon digging through sea glass and making something good and beautiful. Instead, I power up the laptop. After the fiasco at the decoy-painting meeting, it's clear I don't belong in Kennedy Green's do-gooder world. So the sooner I finish her list, the better for all mankind.

And turtles.

I call up a website for endangered turtles and start bucket-list item number three: *Adopt an endangered leatherback turtle in each of my grandparents' names*. This is clearly a twofer.

In a single bucket-list item, Kennedy gets to memorialize her grandparents *and* help save an endangered species. Double the do-gooding, which I'm learning is so Kennedy.

Below me, footsteps clatter on the ladder to the laundry room, and Pen's head pops through the open space in the floor. "I need the laptop."

I browse the turtle adoption page and find leatherback turtles, which are not attractive. They have ridged, cowhidelike backs and old-man faces. I click the "Adopt Now" button.

An irritated snort comes from Pen's direction. "Now!"

An order page replaces the ugly-turtle image. "Use the computer in the kitchen," I tell Penelope's head.

"Mom's updating her website with client testimonials. She'll be on there for hours."

"Five more minutes, and I'll be done." I scroll down the screen, and the ugliness continues. Each leatherback turtle adoption costs one hundred dollars.

"Reb, I need to e-mail information to the track team for the meet tomorrow. I need to get this done now. It's important."

"*This* is important." I go back to the main turtle page and click on other turtles. Adoption for loggerheads will set me back fifty dollars each, desert tortoises only twenty-five dollars. But Kennedy's list specifically mentions leatherback turtles. I grind my knuckles against the sides of my head.

Pen stomps up the ladder and leans her hip against my drafting table. "Sea turtles? Are you doing drugs?"

I click back to the leatherback turtle page. "Yes, the really, really bad ones."

"Since when do you care about sea turtles?"

"They're endangered. Keeps me awake most nights." For the first time, I look Pen in the eye. "If you shut up for five minutes, I can finish this, and you, me, and the poor little turtles can be free of each other."

Assuming Kennedy Green has four grandparents, I'll need to dish out four hundred dollars. Maybe I'll luck out, and a few of Kennedy's grandparents are dead.

Really?

Late-afternoon light, heavy and golden, pours into the attic's dormer windows. I bite back a growl. The truth is, Kennedy would want all four grandparents memorialized, even if they're in a golden heaven. If I'm going to do this right, I need to do the list items in the *spirit* Kennedy intended.

I need four stupid turtles. After buying new tires for the Vespa last month, I have one hundred and twenty-five dollars in my savings account. I select one adoptee named Ernesto.

Pen leaves my table and walks to the back wall of my studio, her fingers trailing along a frame of blue and green glass.

"Hands off," I say. Ernesto has acne and a lazy right eye.

Pen nudges the frame, and it shifts, dangling at a crooked angle. "You know, it's bad enough that you're decorating the walls with trash, but it's creepy to have all these picture frames hanging with no pictures."

"I said, hands off." Ernesto lives near Costa Rica. I hope he has three brothers I can adopt once I get my hands on more money.

"But you don't have any pictures to put in your junky little frames, do you? Not of friends, not of family. Not even a picture of your mom." She jostles another frame. "Or your dad."

The blow catches me fast and hard, midchest.

Pen, a track-team standout, loves competing and winning, and she takes great delight in besting me in the I-have-more-than-you-do game. On her particularly vicious days she plays the father card. My dad was a French Canadian journalist my mother spent one night with in Buenos Aires. She knew only his first name and that he was in town doing a story on the city's art museums. By the time she knew she was pregnant, he was long gone. "He was quite the nomad," Mom had told me. "Always chasing the next story." When I was younger I wondered if he had known about me if he would have stayed. And after Mom died I dreamed about him coming to free me from the bungalow.

"You don't need anyone to make it in this world," Mom often told me. "The power to be extraordinary comes from within."

And she was right. Mom was the most extraordinary person I'd ever known. She won major photography awards, and her work appeared on greeting cards and in magazines and ads all over the world. But more than money and awards, she had a fire for everything she did. I remember one time when we were in the Sea of Cortez and she camped out on a spit of rock for three days where a large school of flying stingrays had been reported. I sat in the Jeep, watching her brave the blistering sun and heat and gritty wind, eventually capturing a series of shots of the giant fish soaring through the air like eagles. Even to my untrained, eight-year-old eyes, I recognized the photo series for the brilliant work of art it was. Mom never sold the rights to the photos, and I understood why. She wasn't ready to give up that piece of her heart.

And for as long as I could remember, Mom told me to follow my heart. "Don't just march to the beat of your own drummer, Reb. March to the beat of your own 275-member band." I don't know why Pen's mentioning my mom and dad now, other than she's been extra pissy since Kennedy's memorial service. I'm in no mood to get into it with her. I'd already fought with Mr. Phillips and every member of the 100 Club today. With another click, I save Ernesto the Expensive to my bookmarks and hand Pen the laptop. "Go."

My cousin takes the computer and skips down the ladder.

I walk to the back wall and straighten the sea-glass frames.

I bang the rubber mallet on the bag of almonds.

"Um, Rebel?" Macey takes the mallet from my hand. "I need almond crumbs, not almond milk."

The bag of almonds is gushy, gluey. "Sorry."

"I can handle it from here." Macey takes the bag and picks out the pieces I haven't sent to a milky grave.

"How much do you think we can make by selling pies?" During lunch period, I'd once again followed Macey to the FACS kitchen, where she made another pie, this one with a graham-cracker crust, almond filling, and blueberries.

"You're getting way too obsessed with this turtle thing." Macey pounds the almonds in a steady, even manner. "I'm assuming the donation jar in the biology lab is your doing."

Heat rises to my face. Dorky, but my deed. I took one of my Mason jars, painted it blue, and made a sea-glass mosaic in the shape of a sea turtle. I attached a sign that read *Save the Endangered Leatherback Turtles*, and cut a slice in the plastic lid. In two days I'd raised twenty-two dollars and fifty-six cents and a wad of dried gum. "It's on the list."

Macey sprinkles the crushed almonds over the blueberries.

Money has never been overly important in my world, at least not amassing large sums of it. To Aunt Evelyn's horror, I prefer army-surplus pants and T-shirts and dime-store flip-flops. I don't need expensive electronic gadgets. I don't covet trendy clothes or designer cell-phone covers.

"After taking out the cost of ingredients, we could make about five dollars per pie." Macey bites into a forkful of pie, her mouth and eyes pinched in concentration. With a sigh, she drops the fork into the sink. "But they're not right. Something's off."

Like my life. Ever since that day in detention, my world has been off-kilter. I'm doing good deeds, hanging out with Mr. Perfect, and worrying about money. As I help Macey clean up, I ponder selling blood, plasma, and hair.

No, not hair. Most people don't get the blue. I discovered the electric-blue dye three years ago at Bella's Discount Beauty Supply, and it reminded me of the blue waters of Belize, a place of sun and warmth and my mom.

The bell rings as Macey puts away the final dish, and I hang the dish towel on the oven door. Out in the hallway, bodies move out of our way. It's one of the perks of wearing a bag with a row of fossilized shark teeth. We leave the crowded hallway and escape into the breezeway. In front of Unit Five Nate hangs out with the other sportos. A girl with big cow eyes bats her lashes at him, clearly one of his admirers from the herd. He doesn't acknowledge me, nor I, him. I don't speak moo.

The tardy bell rings, and students hurry into their class-rooms. I take my time. I have art with Miss Chang, and I have no tardies. Macey doesn't seem in any hurry, either. We reach my locker, and I dig out my art folder.

"Maybe I should try a shortbread crust." Macey rolls her bottom lip between her thumb and forefinger. "Or a crust made with lard. All the fat leaves the crust extra flaky."

"Flaky is good," I say, wondering about her pie obsession, but I don't bother to ask. After the past three school years of being detention comrades and more-or-less friends-of-convenience, I've learned Macey doesn't do personal. She prefers to lurk in the shadows and hide behind her hoodie.

The door at the end of the hall swings open, and Nate rushes into the corridor. Ms. Cow Eyes must have distracted him too long. When he sees Macey and me, his feet skid to a stop. He shifts his backpack to his other shoulder and tilts his chin toward me. "What are you doing Friday afternoon?"

I grab my sketchbook from my locker. I want to show Miss Chang some of my new sea-glass mosaic ideas. "I have an accordion lesson."

The right side of Nate's mouth quirks. "On Friday I plan to set up the decoys at the nesting site on the mudflats. Meet me at five o'clock in the north beach parking lot."

Nate's confidence borders on arrogance, and it irritates me. "And what if I don't want to meet you at five?"

Nate's eyes flash. "You do." He places a palm on the lockers on either side of me. He's a foot taller, and I have to crane my neck to look him in the eye. His mouth curves, and I spot something that looks suspiciously like dimples on either side of his mouth. "And feel free to bring your accordion." The smile deepens. Definitely dimples—more like craters.

My sketchbook clatters to the ground, the sound echoing in the empty hallway.

Tapping the lockers on either side of mine, Nate winks and shoves off.

Macey stares with disbelieving eyes as Nate rushes down

the hall and into the calculus room. "You're going on a date with *him*?"

"It's a community-service project." I slam my locker and snatch my sketchbook from the ground. "We're sticking rubber birds on mudflats."

Macey makes an *uh-huh* sound.

"It's not a date," I insist as we walk down the corridor.

On silent feet, she ducks through the study-hall door.

"It's not a date!"

7. Shoot a flaming arrow

CHAPTER
EIGHT

TREES ARE EVIL. SO ARE THE PEOPLE WHO SELL them.

I swallow my contempt for all things green and step up to the cash register at The Garden Spot. "I'd like to speak to the manager, please."

The clerk, who wears an apron covered with giant sunflowers, looks me up and down, from blue streaks to mud-caked flip-flops, which weren't muddy until my trek through Mr. Green Thumb's back lot.

"We're not hiring," the clerk says.

"I'm not here about a job. I need to talk to the manager about a school project. It's about trees."

After school today I started roaming the streets of downtown Tierra del Rey in search of trees to complete the next item on Kennedy's bucket list: *Plant seedlings in Brazil to replenish our dwindling rain forests.* I can't travel to Brazil, but with a little creativity, I can complete this item in the *spirit* of what Kennedy wanted. Plant more trees. Save the planet.

The problem, thanks to my turtle shopping spree, is I have no money to buy trees, which leads to the inevitable question: *What would Kennedy do?* I swear I should have *WWKD* tattooed on my right forearm. I imagine Kennedy would craft toe rings out of recycled newspaper to earn money or go door-to-door with a juice can. In other words, she'd get others to pony up the cash for the trees. So I've spent the past two hours trying to get plant people to part with a few twigs. The arbor world has not been kind.

The Garden Spot clerk picks up the phone and fifteen seconds later gives me a too-bad-so-sad face. "The manager is busy. She asked me to help you."

Story time. "I'm collecting trees to plant in the parking lot at the Del Rey School near our gym. A few years ago the old trees caught a fungus and died. Percy Cole, who heads our school's maintenance program, wants to plant new trees, but there's no money in the budget. Trees make sense in a school parking lot, combating all that exhaust and keeping young lungs healthy." I show more teeth. Kennedy would love this. "So I'm looking for a plant nursery to donate the trees. We can even include a plaque acknowledging The Garden Spot's donation." And they all lived happily ever after.

"We love supporting our community, but we just gave a large donation to the senior center for their summer garden."

"I don't need a ton of trees."

"I'm sorry."

"One." Kennedy mentioned nothing about quantity.

"Not today."

"Please." I'm begging. *Do you see this, Kennedy? I'm begging for you.*

"Try us around the holidays."

Panic jolts my spine. The holidays are months from now. I can't let this bucket-list thing drag on that long. I thank the unhelpful clerk and take out my phone. I'm hunting for another tree place when I hear, "Yoo-hoo, Rebecca. What in heaven's name are you doing here?"

My eyelids squeeze shut. I don't need Aunt Evelyn. I need trees. Jamming my phone into my pocket, I open my eyes and wave. "Just leaving."

Aunt Evelyn blocks my exit with her cart, which is filled with tiny pots of yellow and purple flowers. "But what were you doing here?"

I don't have time for a smart-ass answer. "I'm trying to get free trees so I can plant them in the north parking lot at school and save planet Earth."

The smooth plane of Aunt Evelyn's forehead creases. "Is

this about drugs, Rebel? Because if you've turned to drugs, there are places and people—"

"I'm not doing drugs." I explain about my tree-planting project.

"You're serious?"

"No. I'm standing here so we can bond."

Aunt Evelyn wears a chin-length bob, sleek and shiny, like a yellow football helmet. The entire helmet now tilts to the right. "That's an interesting project." The football helmet tilts to the other side. "And admirable."

"It would be, if I could get someone to donate the trees," I say more to myself than to her.

Aunt Evelyn clucks her tongue. "You'd have more luck getting donations if you dressed more professionally."

"I need to go." I try to push past her cart, but she jams it into a stack of fertilizer, cutting me off.

"I know you have your own unique and strong style, Rebecca, and I'm not suggesting you change. I actually think it works to your advantage. Your style makes you memorable." She motions to me with rose-tipped fingers, a perfect match for the rosy pearls at her ears. "You don't need to do much. Get rid of the shark teeth, and put on a clean shirt and nice sandals."

"Right, like that's going to get me trees."

"First impressions are crucial. The Taylors' place on Manzanita Way has a long driveway lined with brown bark. Now picture that same winding drive with these pansies greeting potential buyers as they drive to the front entrance. It's all about curb appeal, and frankly, Rebecca, yours is lacking."

"This is so wrong." I leap over the mound of fertilizer.

"Try it," Aunt Evelyn calls as she wheels after me.

"Toodles." I waggle my fingers and—

"Dammit, for once would you do something I tell you!" The football helmet quakes, as if it's coming undone. "Listen, Rebecca, I know about these things. I know about images and perceptions. I know about selling yourself and a concept."

"I'm so happy for you."

She smooths both sides of her hair. "Watch."

I want to storm off, but I stay rooted in place. A sick part of me can't wait for her to fail, but I desperately need trees, so I'm sort of rooting for her.

Aunt Evelyn walks back to the sunflower clerk at the register. She swishes her football helmet, starts chatting, and two minutes later, a woman in a green apron with mud splatters joins her at the register. Ten minutes later Aunt Evelyn and I are the proud owners of ten Red Rocket crepe myrtle trees donated by The Garden Spot.

As she wheels them to her van, Aunt Evelyn wears her I-told-you-so face, the one she dons when she demonstrates that I wear the wrong clothes, say the wrong words, and dream the wrong dreams. It's been Aunt Evelyn's MO for five years.

Look, Rebecca, you're the only girl at the birthday party not *wearing a dress. Don't you feel out of place?*

I told you, Rebecca, to study more. Now your summer is going to be ruined because you have to spend most of it in summer school retaking math.

See, Rebecca, if you get rid of your blue hair, shark teeth, and flip-flops, you'll get yourself ten Red Rocket crepe myrtle trees.

On Friday afternoon I drive Nova to the Del Rey Nature Preserve. Pulling into the parking lot, I cut Nova's engine, dig into my messenger bag, and pull out a cigarette. I light up and take a long draw as I wait for Nate.

You're going on a date with him?

No, Macey, I'm not, because Nate doesn't date girls with blue hair. He's a baseball-team superstar and member of the football team, National Honor Society, 100 Club, student government, and crew. He was on last year's homecoming and Mistletoe courts and dated a Cupcake. I know because I took out Pen's yearbook from last year and looked.

Pretty creepy, huh?

No, Kennedy, I'm not a creeper. I want to know more about Nate because I will be spending an inordinate amount of time with him, possibly up to a hundred hours, and it's best to know your enemies. I pull in another long, sweet breath of nicotine, the muscles in my neck relaxing. That's not right. Nate Bolivar is not the enemy. He has looks and brains and is probably the proud owner of a Mr. Congeniality trophy or two. In all of Nate's yearbook photos he's smiling, confident, the picture of perfection. While I don't care about racking up wins or starring on a team, the Nates of this world do, which makes us fundamentally different. People like me don't work toward perfection in an imperfect world. We celebrate imperfection.

A bright red Mustang convertible pulls into the parking lot, but Nate is not at the wheel. Bronson hangs a sharp right and parks next to my scooter. Something in my stomach dips. Of course Bronson is here. This isn't a date but a community-service project.

Nate climbs out of the passenger side of the sports car and lets out a wolf whistle. "Nice wheels."

"Nate, meet Nova. Nova, this is Nate."

"Does it run?" Bronson asks with a curl of his lip.

I return the snarl. "Only if I sing it sappy love songs from the eighties."

Nate runs a hand along the Vespa's case. "Start her up."

I twist the ignition, and Nova coughs, sputters, and hums six out of every eight notes.

"Sounds like a carburetor issue," Nate says.

"So you're a straight-A student, Mr. Baseball, president of the Bleeding Hearts Club, and a scooter whisperer?"

"No, my dad's a mechanic. He refuses to teach me anything about cars." Nate's lips twist in a devilish curve. "But I watch over his shoulder."

I would have loved to have learned about art from my father. As for Mom, she tried to teach me about lenses and shutter speeds, but I never could wrap my head around the numbers and angles, not that she cared. She saw that I'd rather capture the world with a pencil or crayons. "Follow your passions, Reb, no one else's," Mom told me on more than one occasion.

"Let's go." Bronson takes out a canvas bag with the decoys and two shovels. "Some of us have lives. And can you put out that thing?" He aims a shovel at my cigarette. "You smell like an ashtray."

I open my mouth and then snap it closed. Nate's still standing at my shoulder, ogling Nova. My ashtray breath will clash with his fresh-out-of-the-shower scent. I stub out the cigarette on a rock wall and put the butt into the plastic bag tied to one of my belt loops.

Nate takes the shovels, and we trek along the boardwalk, past the dunes with sea grass to the rocky part of the beach. Bronson drones on about some special football camp he's attending at the beginning of summer, and Nate asks the occasional question. Every so often I find a bottle cap or straw or cigarette butt and slip it into my trash bag.

When we reach a set of tide pools, Nate slows. "Look, there's a limpet." He squats and peers into a shallow pool. "And here's a wooly sculpin fish."

"And look there," I say with a squeal. "It's a gum wrapper." I dislodge the paper wedged between a pair of rocks and tuck it into my trash bag. "Score!"

Nate laughs, a nice, rumbly sound much like the ocean

rushing the rocky tide pools. He seems less intense out here, not so uptight.

Bronson balances on a pair of rocks. "No one thinks you're funny, Rebel. Actually, the entire school thinks you're a loser."

I shouldn't. Deep in my heart, I know I shouldn't. "Maybe I should start an after-school club for losers, and you can be vice president."

Nate shakes the water from his hands. "Let's get to the mudflats."

"No," Bronson says. "I'm not going to put up with this crap all afternoon." He drops the bag of bird decoys. "I'm tired of your snide comments."

"Would you prefer snarky over snide?" I ask with feigned politeness.

"I'd prefer you leave."

And this, dear Kennedy, is why I don't belong in your world. Most people don't get me. I'm not a square peg in a round hole; I'm a trapezoid. "Nate invited me."

"Because he felt sorry for you."

I spot a beer-bottle cap and toss it into my bag. "Sorry? For me?"

Nate stands. "Bronson, knock it off."

"Nope, I'm going to give it right back at her." Bronson jabs a sausage finger at me. "You have no friends, and you're always making stupid, snarky comments. Nate thinks you're lonely and you mouth off to get attention."

"Lonely? Your bicep is bigger than your brain. Just because I don't aspire to hang out with the in-crowd doesn't mean I'm lonely."

"Oh yeah? Name one friend."

Nate slicks back his hair, which is pointless because not a strand is out of place. "Bronson—"

I gesture to cut off Nate. "No, let Mr. Head-up-His-Ass speak."

"You're psychotic. And pathetic."

"And you're an idiot."

"Yep, I am. Or at least I was on the day I agreed to do this project with *you*. Nate, I can't deal with this today. I'm going to go destroy weeds." He grabs one of the shovels and storms off.

I raise my hand to give him a wiggly send-off, but my fingers tremble. I tuck them into my back pockets instead. Above us a seagull cries, and something swishes in the tide pool.

Nate lowers himself to the pool. "I'm sorry he said those things."

"You shouldn't apologize."

"His girlfriend dumped him this morning. He's not mad at you. He's mad at everyone with two X chromosomes."

"You feel responsible for his boneheaded actions?"

"No, but I understand why he's on edge. Still, his comments were out of line." Nate points to the far edge of the pool. "Pink algae."

I squat to get a closer look at pink slime. Instead I see my face, an odd, chalky white color reflected in the sunlit water. I shift from one foot to the other. "Do you agree with him?"

"I never called you psychotic and pathetic." Nate nudges a submerged rock, and something scuttles through the water. "That's an opaleye fish."

The swish of the fish elongates my face, and my mouth distorts as if in midscream. "But you called me a loner."

"I called you *lonely*." He settles the rock back into place. "There's a difference."

"I'm not lonely. I'm not feeling little tugs on my heartstrings to swap friendship bracelets." I have Macey and my fellow delinquents, but I shouldn't have to list my friends to prove I have them. I dip my hand into the sun-soaked water and nudge a different rock. "Feeling lonely would indicate I have an unrealized need for people."

"Everyone needs people, Reb."

We all need friends.

I push harder on the rock. Heaven forbid I forget Kennedy for five minutes. "But I'm not everyone, am I?"

You, Rebel Blue, are anything but ordinary.

Nate rocks back on his heels. The sun glints off his shiny, blue-black hair. "No, Rebel, you're not."

I can't tell if that's a criticism or a compliment. Not that it matters what Nate thinks of me. I jump to my feet and shake off the water.

On our way to the sea swallows' nesting site at the mudflats, we cross an outcrop of rocks. "This time of day, we may see a pod of dolphins straight ahead," Nate says. He shades his eyes with one hand and scans the ocean. His eyes are bright, his cheeks flushed. I bet this is how I look flying down the hill on Nova.

"You love it out here, don't you?" I ask.

"I need plenty of community-service hours if I'm going to get a full-ride scholarship to college."

"Liar."

He drops his hand to his side. "Not that again."

"If you lie, I'm going to call you on it." I motion to the sea and sky. "This isn't just about helping endangered birds. You love being out here."

"You don't have a filter, do you?"

"I find them rather unnecessary." I wiggle my toes. "Like shoes."

He raises his face to the sky and takes a deep breath of the salty breeze, his faded Del Rey School baseball T-shirt stretching across his chest. "Okay, I love it out here."

I cup my hand to my ear. "Excuse me, what's that?"

Nate shakes his head, a reluctant smile snaking onto his mouth. "You're right. There, I said it. Does that make you happy?"

"If I had pom-poms, I'd be shaking them."

We stand side by side, watching the water and sky. "See that out there?" He points to the gentle swell of ocean to our right.

I squint at the deep blue waves dotted with tiny whitecaps. "What?"

"The sailboat. It's a twenty-five-foot Hunter with a teak deck and bobblehead dolphin doll hanging from the captain's wheel."

"What are you talking about? I don't see a boat and bobble-head."

"You will next summer, and I'll be behind the wheel, headed for the Baja." His grin turns into a laugh as I thwack him on the shoulder, which is hard as a boulder but oddly warm.

I jab my hand into my pants pocket.

"Look!" Nate points to a different part of the ocean. "There's a dolphin—two—no, three."

I snort and head for the mudflats just past the rock. "Sure, Nate, right next to your sailboat."

He takes my hand and drags me to the edge of the cliff. "Wait a minute and . . . and . . ." A seagull flies overhead, and somewhere in the mudflats a bird twitters. Nate nestles his arm against mine, moving our hands in a slow sweep. ". . . and . . . and . . . now!"

Three silver arcs fly from the water in front of our nestled arms. I stumble back. My bare foot lands in a small hole. I lunge forward to keep from falling. Frothy water churns and pounds the rocks twenty feet below the cliff. A scream tears up my throat. Hands tighten around my waist and pull.

Nate and I tumble backward, his body curling around mine.

The sky cartwheels. Nate lands on a patch of earth covered in purple and white wildflowers. I land on him. No more cliff. Just Nate.

My chest rises and falls with his. We share a breath. The sweet smell of crushed flowers rises, overpowering the salt sea.

"Am I interrupting something?" Bronson asks.

"No!" I jump off Nate as if I'd touched an electric eel.

Nate's slower. He stands, swatting crushed leaves and sand from his shorts. "Rebel got too close to the edge. I pulled her back. We lost our balance."

"That's right," I say. "We lost our balance."

8. Start a fire without matches

CHAPTER
NINE

DOWNSTAIRS, THE MUSIC BLASTS, AND THE GLASS frames rattle on the back wall of my attic studio. I cram Percy's earplugs into my ears and try to do math.

Attorney fees + IRS application fees > cost of adopting four leatherback turtles.

I rub at my temples and wonder how I'm going to get the money for the next item on Kennedy Green's bucket list: *Start my own 501(c)(3) charity.*

As I thumb through the papers and read about bylaws, boards of directors, tax ID numbers, and IRS guidelines, I realize Kennedy Green is more annoying dead than alive.

On the floor below, someone shrieks, and then something

clanks and crashes. It's probably one of Aunt Evelyn's ceramic roosters. Uncle Bob and Aunt Evelyn drove to San Diego for the night because Aunt Evelyn has an early-morning open house there tomorrow. It's Saturday night, and Pen and the Cupcakes are having a party.

I read about mission statements and visions, but the words shimmy and shake in time with the music. Tiberius, the next-door neighbor's rat terrier, starts to bark.

I pull the plugs from my ears because I'm not going to be able to get anything done tonight. And, honestly, I've had enough of Kennedy's bucket list today. The latest stumbling block: School administration threw a fit when I brought the Red Rocket trees to school this morning. Apparently I hadn't acquired them through an approved vendor, nor did I fill out the proper paperwork for "supply acquisition."

"I just want to do something good," I told the principal.

Percy stepped in and said he'd take care of the paperwork. On Monday I plan to give Percy one of Macey's pies. *Yoo-hoo, Bronson, another friend.*

Downstairs in the land of Cupcakes, I duck past a boisterous group playing Twister and weave through another half dozen of Penelope's friends lounging in the kitchen eating pizza and jelly beans. I stop at the counter and grab a piece of pizza. After downing it, I dig through the jelly beans, picking out the black ones. No one says a word. With jelly beans in hand, I walk out the back door onto the porch.

Tiberius pokes his head through a new hole under the fence. His ears tilt forward, and his crooked teeth flash in his version of a smile. I hop over the porch railing and toss him the jelly beans. He lunges, snapping up the sugary treats with gnashing teeth.

Then I follow the sound of waves.

Tonight bonfires dot the beach. Tongues of flames lick the inky sky, and in the back of my head a new design takes shape, a mosaic with elongated bits of amber and yellow sea glass, maybe on a black frame. I stroll along the boardwalk, past the sand, past the people. At the back of the grassy dunes a lone man reclines on a piece of cardboard. He smells of ripe sweat and rich earth. With his matted hair and scarecrow arms, he's probably homeless, but he must find solace in this place of shifting sea. He rocks back and forth to the music of the ocean.

I pick my way past the tide pools and climb toward the outcrop of rocks. I try not to picture Nate putting his arm around me and pointing out the dolphins. I try not to remember falling through the air and landing in his arms. I try not to feel the brush of his breath on my skin. Slipping through the craggy rocks, I search the sea. Maybe I'll see dolphins or whales or glow-in-the-dark algae, because now would be a good time to stop obsessing about Nate. As I near the point, one of the boulders shifts. It's not a rock but a person. In profile I make out neat hair, a square chin, and chiseled nose. And if the moon were brighter, I'd spot two curving dimples.

It's fate.

I spin and tiptoe back across the rocks.

"Got another pod of dolphins out there," Nate calls.

I run the toe of my flip-flop along a pile of rocks. I could pretend I didn't hear him. But why? So we *breathed* together. So he makes me jump and leaves me off balance. I can't deny that, but I also know that boys like Nate prefer to *breathe* with girls from the herd.

I join Nate on the cliff and take a seat on a smooth rock. Squinting, I spot dorsal fins. It's hard to tell in the blue-black sea of rolling velvet, but there are six, maybe seven. I pull my knees to my chest, breathing in the quiet. Nate says nothing. I picture his huge, chatty family. Like me, he probably came to escape the noise. Or maybe he was doing work at the mudflats nearby. The sea swallows are expected within a week or two, and through the moonlight I see our newly erected fence posts.

Nate doesn't say what brought him to this chunk of rock, and I don't ask. We sit side by side and watch the sea. Like me, he seems content with the company of the waves and wind. At one point he settles onto his back, his intertwined fingers under his head. When the moon peeks out from a thin cover of clouds, the moonlight brightens our perch. I notice Nate's shirt is from a 5K to raise money for juvenile diabetes.

I idly trace a series of wavy lines in the fine layer of sand dusting the rock. "So if you wanted to start a charity, how would you do it?"

He rolls to his side and raises himself on a bent arm. Moonlight and shadow play over the waves of his hair. "The bucket list?"

I flick a small pebble with my fingernail, and it sails over the edge into blackness. "What do you think?"

"Sounds like something Kennedy Green would have wanted to do before she died."

"Where do I start?"

"With something you care about. Tia Mina would call them your passions."

My passions. I hug my knees to my chest. There's so much I want to do and see, so much that can't be done chained to a school desk or in a single town on the edge of the ocean. "Art. I love art. I draw, paint, and make mosaics out of sea glass. I love my Vespa and traveling and finding new places. And freedom. I'm passionate about freedom to speak my mind and follow my dreams. I'm passionate about the freedom to be me."

"You're getting deep."

"The more time you spend thinking about something, the deeper you get into your heart." Great, now I'm channeling my creepy detention supervisor. "Forget I said that last bit." Time to shut my mouth. I scrutinize the beach in the distance, surprised most of the bonfires are out. "What time is it?"

Nate holds his watch to the moonlight and squints. "Eleven thirty. Why?"

"Crap! I only have thirty minutes."

"To do what?"

"A random act of kindness."

"It has to be done now?"

"Before midnight." It slipped my mind, but it shouldn't have. It's Nate, of course. He's distracting. I scramble off the rock.

"What are you going to do?" Nate asks as he follows me through the grassy dunes.

"Not sure. I've already done the clean-the-beach thing." At this time of night there's not much going on, and there's no one on this part of the beach but the homeless man.

"Do you need a ride? My dad's truck is over there."

Mr. White Knight to the rescue. We dive into an ancient truck with rounded wheel wells and running boards. He cranks the ignition a half dozen times before it coughs and roars to life. "Where to?"

"Head toward downtown on Calle Bonita. Maybe I'll find a little old lady who needs help crossing the street."

I don't see a single gray hair but after two blocks spot an all-night grocery store. A man pushes a shopping cart through the parking lot. "Pull in there," I tell Nate. When Nate stops, I jump out of the truck. "Hey, let me give you a hand."

"I got 'em." The man has beefy arms and a gut that hangs over his belt.

I settle my hands on his cart, which is filled with twelve-packs of beer. "I want to help."

He swats me away, as if I'm a mosquito. "Get out of here, kid. I ain't giving you no beer."

"I don't want any beer." I reach for one of the twelve-packs. "I just want to do something nice for my fellow man." Something crunches behind me, and I spin just as a little old lady bats a beaded purse against my head. I grab my right ear and yelp.

"Got her, Buddy!" The old lady raises her arm again.

The beer guy grabs her arm. "It's okay, Mom. She's leaving."

He gives me a bearlike growl, and I hurry back to Nate's truck where he's rubbing his chin and trying not to laugh. "That didn't go well."

I rub my ear. "Start driving."

A half block down the street we pass a brightly lit restaurant. Mariachi music floats from the patio, where a waiter carries a large tray of food to a pair of late-night customers. "There! Pull into Dos Hermanas." I run inside the Mexican cantina and shout to the woman at the register, "Two street tacos to go!"

"Beef or chicken?"

"Whatever's fastest."

The woman tilts her head as if she doesn't understand English, and Nate leans in close and winks. "It's a taco emergency."

Within four minutes I have two steamy chicken tacos and a side of guacamole. "Back to the beach—hurry!"

Nate punches the accelerator. We squeal out of the parking

lot toward the ocean. When we arrive at the grassy dunes, I point to the road's shoulder. "Pull over there."

Once out of the truck, I rush through the grass and past the lifeguard tower where I spotted the homeless man.

"Here!" I thrust the tacos into his face.

He backs away from the bag as if it were a live snake. "What's that?"

"Tacos."

He scratches at a tuft of greasy, matted hair poking from the side of his head. "What's it for?"

"You." I wave the bag, sending curls of charred-meat-and-onion steam through the air.

He squints at me through a sun-roughened face. "You on drugs?"

"I am not doing drugs. Why does everyone think I'm doing drugs?" I take a long breath. "Listen, I'm trying to do something kind." I turn back to Nate. "What time is it?"

"Eleven fifty-eight."

"Just take the tacos."

The man licks his lips, and I wonder when he last ate. Something scampers through the grassy dunes. Remnants of laughter echo from the beach far below us.

"Please," I whisper.

Bronson's right. I'm pathetic.

After checking his watch again, Nate takes the bag from my hand. "I got this." He sets the bag on the corner of the cardboard, grabs my hand, and pulls me away. I'm about to kick sand at him when paper rustles behind us. I turn just as the man shoves one of the tacos into his mouth. Juice dribbles down his chin as he snatches the other taco. I jog away, too embarrassed to stick around.

Next to me Nate makes a snuffling sound. His shoulders jiggle. My lips twitch. By the time we climb back into the truck, we're laughing out loud.

"Check." Nate positions his fingers as if holding a pencil and makes a check mark in the air. "One random act of kindness."

"More like random act of weirdness." I raise my face to the night sky. "This is crazy."

"But crazy in a good way."

Yes, it felt good. Kennedy would have approved. I settle against the cracked leather seat in the old truck. "By the way, you broke the law."

"What?"

"You sped."

"Did not."

"You drove eleven miles over the speed limit on the way to the beach. I checked the speedometer as we passed the cop car sitting in the convenience-store parking lot."

He grimaces. "Those tickets aren't cheap."

I rest my elbow on the edge of the open window. "You shouldn't spend so much time with me. I'm a bad influence."

"True," he says with another shake of his shoulders.

When we reach my street, the bungalow is still filled with Cupcakes, but now they have company. Three new cars are parked out front. Nate finds a spot near the neighbor's house, and I weigh the wisdom of spending the night with Tiberius. I reach for the door handle, but Nate locks his fingers around my wrist. I start to pull away, and he lets up, the touch softening until it's just the featherlight brush of his fingertips against the top of my hand.

My heart beats triple-time, and the blood courses through my veins so hard, I can almost see it pulsing in the top of my hand. When I look up from our hands, I see Nate's face, more puzzled than pained or impassioned. He looks very un-Nate-like, as if he's not sure who I am or what to do with me.

It's a good thing for both of us that I recognize the truth about this disturbing collision of our worlds. "Nate, I'm not your kind of girl," I say, not unkindly.

He turns my hand over, so we're palm to palm. The bewildered look gives way to something warmer. He inches closer, simultaneously pulling me toward him. "Shouldn't I be the one to decide who my kind of girl is?"

"I don't like shoes."

"You have cute toes." A dimple appears.

Shit. "I'm disruptive in math and don't play nicely in sandboxes."

"I'll have my little brother say a Rosary for your soul." Another dimple.

"Nate, I'm being serious."

"Me, too." His eyes are a dark, steamy chocolate, every hair on his head in place. Everything about Nate is perfect. He's charming, smart, kind. Everyone likes him. And that's the problem. I'm not everyone. I'm not good at sharing paint. I don't know about tree-acquisition rules. I'm not one of the herd.

His fingers twine with mine. The heat must be burning off all the oxygen in the cab of the truck, because I'm light-headed.

A pair of headlights slashes across the windshield. Bronson pulls up in his red Mustang, which is filled with Nate's sporto buddies. The muscles in Nate's hand tense and harden. The Mustang lets loose a loud honk. Nate drops my hand and slides back to the driver's side.

My lungs expand, and finally oxygen rushes to my brain.

I lunge for the passenger-side door. Nate doesn't reach for me. Instead he stares at the roof liner of the truck. "Let me walk you to the door. It's getting late." No more dimples. No more steamy eyes. Welcome back, Mr. Polite and Proper.

He's also an ass.

I shake my head at my own asslike behavior. "I'm in a made-for-cable teen-angst movie."

"Excuse me?"

I jerk my hand toward the Mustang. "You're embarrassed to be seen with me."

"Why would you think that?"

My fingers fumble along the truck door for the handle. "On

a deserted rocky shore or the dark cab of a pickup truck I'm fine for a quick grab and feel, but when your buddies show, I'm not the right kind of girl." I find the handle and yank. The door groans open, and I stumble out of the truck.

9. Pole dance on the North Pole for Santa's elves

CHAPTER
TEN

NOVA WON'T GO, SO I WALK TO THE BEACH.

This morning there will be no dolphin watching or working on the sea-swallow nesting site. Either would be a bad choice, as I might run into Nate. Running into Nate would mean I'd have to talk to Nate, and I'm not sure what I'd say to him.

We're two separate species, Nate. You're a member of Sporto Popularus, *and I'm classified as* Art Nerd Rebelum. *No intermingling of species.*

Or . . . *When you lace your fingers with mine in a whisper of a touch, my heart booms and my pulse pounds, and I can't breathe, therefore risking death by asphyxiation.*

Or the ever popular and appropriate . . . *Asshole.*

Which is why I'm walking to the beach in search of the Del Rey Fun and Sun Rental Shop. Every item on the top half of Kennedy's bucket list is of the do-gooder variety, and after last night in the truck with Nate, I decided I needed a break from good. This morning I skip to: *Ride a bicycle built for two.*

Business is hopping at the Fun and Sun Rental Shop this sunny Sunday morning.

"I'd like to rent a tandem bike," I tell the woman behind the counter.

"Sorry, I rented out our last tandem about half an hour ago. Can I interest you in a beach cruiser, caster board, or unicycle? We have so many choices."

"No, thanks."

I try Beach Bikes and Beyond, Toby & Trey's Bike Emporium, and Cheap Wheels. All rent tandems, but all are sold out. The Del Rey boardwalk stretches three miles along the Pacific Ocean, and I stop at every shop that rents things with wheels. At mile two, one of my flip-flops breaks, and I toss them into the trash.

Near the end of the boardwalk I enter Bubba's Beach Bikes. The handwritten sign on the front window notes he's already out of beach cruisers, but Bubba assures me he has a tandem bike he'll rent to me for two hours. "And I'll knock the price down to ten bucks because it's in pretty bad shape. Salty sea air rusts stuff."

Bubba, a skinny guy with a long face and carrot-colored hair, wheels the bike out of the back room. Both seats are cracked and split, and rusty dots pit the frame.

"Perfect," I say.

Bubba takes my money and wheels the bike, which squeaks like Aunt Evelyn on one of her bad-hair days, onto the boardwalk. "Okay, Captain," he says. "Where's your stoker?"

"My what?"

"Your back rider. I need to give you both a few tips. You each play different roles on a tandem. Your stoker is your power on climbs, but he can also throw off your equilibrium. You need to work together on weight shifts, pedal force, and coasting. Tandem riding is all about teamwork. It's about two riders becoming one."

Who knew tandem bikes had so many rules? "I don't have a stoker."

He scratches the orange soul patch on his chin. "But you want a tandem bike?"

"Yes."

"That's weird."

"Welcome to my world."

Bubba looks at me as if I'm crazy but finishes the tandem lesson and sends me on my way.

I have no idea why Kennedy wanted to ride a tandem bike before she died. Maybe her film crush rode a tandem with the love of his life in her favorite movie, or maybe she never rode a bike because she was afraid of falling and needed someone at her side to help her conquer her fear. But I do know that a person's past affects the choices she makes in the present and for the future. Case in point: As a kid I never caught on to math, so in the future I will not choose to be an accountant.

So what kind of past makes a person want to do a random act of kindness every day for a year? Did Kennedy grow up in a family of do-gooders, or was she desperately in need of kindness because there was none in her world? My fingers curl around the gearshift. But the why doesn't matter. The important thing is that I complete the list.

Pretty soon I'm cruising and squeaking along the beach walk. This tandem stuff is a piece of cake, no different from riding a regular bike and much easier than adopting four leatherback turtles and starting my own charity. But according to Bubba, tandem riding is all about teamwork . . . two riders becoming one.

I want to do things right, you know?

I growl so loudly, a woman on a bike with a kiddie carrier swerves out of my way.

So I need a stoker. My choices are few. Cousin Pen? She'd brake just to make me work harder. Uncle Bob? In San Diego. Nate? Won't go there.

Then it hits me. I know just who to ask.

My sophomore year a boy from detention invited me to a party at his house. While there, I ran into Macey, who said she lived a few doors down. At the party Macey and I spent most of the evening sitting on the pool deck with our feet in the water, keeping drunks from peeing into the pool.

I don't remember much about the party at Detention Guy's house, but I do remember he lived off Paseo del Sol. I pedal along the street searching for Macey's house and try to figure out what kind of dwelling houses a teenage grim reaper. No black paint. No gravestones or cypress trees draped with wisps of moss. After I've knocked on two doors, a neighbor informs me the Kellingsworths live in the white house on the corner with lime-green trim and a salsa garden.

"You must be Rebel!" The woman who answers the door wrenches my arm nearly out of its socket as she pulls me into the entryway. "It's so nice to have Macey's best friend over. She told me all about you. How you help with the pies. How you hang out together after school. You're the artist. So talented. I'd love to see your work. Macey's in the kitchen. Would you like pie?"

Macey stands at the kitchen sink, her arms buried in soapy water, two pies cooling on the counter. She wears black shorts and a black T-shirt. It's strange not to see the hoodie hanging from her shoulders.

Macey looks up from the soapy water and drops the bowl she'd been scrubbing.

"Hi," I say with an awkward wave.

Mrs. Kellingsworth stands with her hand clasped to her

chest. "I'll let you two girls chat. I know at this age there's so much to chat about. School and clothes and movies and boys. Chat. Just chat."

"I am so adopted," Macey says to the dishwater after her mother leaves.

"Your mom has nothing on my Aunt Evelyn." Although ever since the procurement of Red Rocket trees, Auntie Ev's been less antagonistic, which has led to a little less snark from my corner of the bungalow.

I pull out a chair at the table and sit. The air in Macey's kitchen is warm and heavy with sweet smells. My nose twitches. "Cinnamon?"

"Nutmeg." Macey gnaws on her bottom lip as she slips the bowl into the drainer and jams her hands back into the soapy water.

"I rented a tandem bike," I say.

She washes two forks.

"I thought maybe you'd like to ride it with me."

She scrapes gunk off a large spoon. "Ride? With you?"

"Yeah."

Measuring cups and spoons clank as she plunges them into the water and shakes her head.

"It's a nice day, and it's fun," I say.

Another head shake.

"Listen, Macey, I *need* to ride a tandem bike with someone."

Macey scrubs at the dishes, rubbing so hard and fast, the

suds multiply. "Ask that guy Nate. He seems to like you."

Only when no one's watching. I picture Nate dropping my hand when he recognized his friends. I feel the coldness spreading across my skin. I get up from the table, grab a dish towel on the counter, and dry the bowl in the drainer. I rub and rub until the cold goes away. "Please, Macey. I need someone to do this with me."

Her hands and the suds grow still. "I can't."

I knot the dish towel around my hands. "Why?"

"I need peaches."

"Peaches? You need peaches?"

The corner of Macey's mouth tilts a fraction, and her eyes brighten. "I need to go to the farmers' market. The first peaches of the season arrive today."

I toss the dish towel onto the counter, tension lifting from my knotted fingers. "I can deal with peaches."

"The hardest thing is starting," I tell Macey, imparting all my newfound tandem wisdom from Bubba the Bike Sage. "Rest your right foot on the pedal, and when I push off, push. Got it?"

Macey looks as if she's about to dive into a tank with Herman the shark, but she nods. Like me, she doesn't seem too thrilled with the whole let's-connect-on-a-bike thing. I don't know much about her life, and for a moment I wonder how she ended up here with me. Maybe she too was homeschooled and missed the lesson on how to play nicely in the sandbox.

Or maybe she had some kind of trauma that made her turn inward. Or maybe it's none of my business.

I push off the bricks around the salsa garden. The tandem lurches forward. Macey and I sway to the right. "Lean left!" I scream. We lean, but not fast enough. We tumble onto Macey's front lawn. "We can do this. We *have* to do this."

I untangle my legs from the bike and stand. Macey lies on the grass, her pale, thin hair spread out like a spiderweb, her mouth curved in a grin. Her teeth are unexpectedly bright. I hold out my hand. She reaches, and the sleeve of her hoodie pulls back and exposes her forearm. My fingers twitch. A series of lines stripe her skin. Some are short and thick, others long and narrow, the width of a few strands of hair. All are the color of old chalk. Macey yanks her sleeve over the scars and scrambles to her feet. A speckled red creeps up her neck.

I haul the bike upright and straddle the frame, facing forward. "Let's try this again. I think we pushed off too slowly."

Behind me Macey remains motionless. In my head I see her on that day in the detention room when Ms. Lungren told us we needed to examine our deadly behaviors and write bucket lists. No wonder Macey bailed. The knife, the razor, the tip of a pen—whatever it was that had caused those scars—could have gone deeper. Maybe it already had.

"Come on," I say. "Let's try again."

"I hurt my knee." Macey's voice is low and breathy, borderline panicky. "I need to get inside."

I picture the sweat on her face as she cuts and dices and mixes, the light in her eyes as she peeks into the oven. I have no idea why Macey's suddenly obsessed with pies, but I know they're important to her. "No, Macey, you need peaches."

At last Macey's sandals pad through the grass, and she gets onto the bike. After one more tumble, we get the tandem into motion. We shift our bodies and maneuver around corners. We brake together and come to a controlled stop. After ten minutes of starts and stops, we're pedaling down the bike path to the farmers' market, our bodies working in tandem.

At a red light, we lower our feet at the same time to balance on the curb. I keep my eyes trained straight ahead. Behind me I feel Macey tugging on her sleeves.

I should say something. Kennedy would know what to say, something thoughtful and encouraging, something straight from a greeting card. The light for cross traffic turns yellow.

But I'm not Kennedy. "Stop kicking yourself in the ass," I tell Macey. "We all fall down. We all have scars. Some are more visible than others, and anyone who tries to deny it is full of bullshit."

I can't see Macey, but on the tandem, we are connected. We feel each other's slightest movements. She nods. The light turns green.

By the time we lock the bike at the rack outside the farmers' market, Macey's cheeks are flushed, but not from embarrassment or shame or anger. She grabs my elbow and squeals. "Look, Rebel! Peaches!"

Macey drags me to a produce stand, where she ogles the rosy, gold mounds of peaches. Her fingers hover over the fruit on the far right, and at last she selects a blushing, perfectly shaped peach and holds it to her nose. She inhales slowly and holds the breath. I hold mine.

Her shoulders slump. "Not ready."

An odd sense of disappointment settles over me as she puts the peach back into the bin. "I'm sorry."

"Me, too," she says in a near-whisper.

On our way out of the farmers' market, we pass a berry vendor. Macey finds two cartons of ripe raspberries, and her mood brightens. By the time we reach the tandem, she is talking about raspberry pie toppings. "I can go with a dark chocolate drizzle or milk chocolate shavings or"—her grin deepens—"white chocolate chunks. What do you think?"

With her flushed cheeks and bright eyes, there's nothing deathly or ghostly about Macey now. "One of each." I unfasten the lock. "So I've been meaning to ask . . . what's up with the pies?"

"It's stupid."

"Says who?"

Macey puts her cartons of raspberries in the tandem basket, rearranging them four times. "I'm experimenting with pies to enter in the Great American Bake-Off." At my look of utter stupefaction, she gets onto the back of the bike. "See? It's stupid."

"No, no, I'm just surprised. Is this a pie-baking contest?"

"Pies, tarts, savory items like quiches. You bake things using certain products, and if you win, you go on national TV and win a bunch of money."

I think of leatherback turtles and application costs for 501 (c)(3) charities. "A bunch of money would be nice."

Macey steadies the bike as I get on. "It's not about the money, Rebel. It's just something I always wanted to do. Crazy, huh?"

"No, not crazy. You're being true to you." Just like Kennedy had had the need to straighten the produce display after she took an apple. Just like I need to wear a streak of blue in my hair to remind me of a happier time and place.

We wheel the tandem to the curb, where we push off and pedal out of the market parking lot, the noise of vendors and shoppers dimming until all I hear is the squeak and rattle of Bubba's bike. Somewhere past Calle Bonita, Macey's feet slow. She fidgets with the handlebars, twisting the grips, which grind and squeak.

"Why don't they bother you?" Macey asks me.

I know she's not talking about peaches or raspberries. "The scars?"

She doesn't say anything, which is answer enough.

"They're faded, a part of your past." I hear Macey's foot slip off the pedal. That was the wrong thing to say. If I were better at the whole friend thing, I'd know the right words. I nibble the inside of my cheek and wonder what Kennedy would do. Easy.

Kennedy would talk. "Do you . . . uh . . . want to talk about it?"

Macey's legs get back in rhythm. "No, not really. I talked about it for two years to a therapist."

"Good. I mean, not that I don't want to talk or anything, just that you talked to someone. I think." I wonder if there's any way I can possibly make this more awkward.

"Most people who see them get hung up or freaked out," Macey says. "When they look at me, all they see are scars."

Down the center of the room I share with Pen is the Continental Divide. On one side of the divide, a half dozen designer pillows are neatly arranged on a matching bedspread, and the only item on the shiny hardwood floor is a color-coordinated throw rug perfectly parallel to the bed skirt. That would *not* be my side. I dig through the detritus poking out from beneath my bed, unearthing a dried set of finger paints and a petrified donut. Underneath an eighth-grade report card I find a pair of sneakers, the plain white kind with boxy toes.

Time for another item on Kennedy's bucket list: *Run a seven-minute mile.*

Pen runs. The Cupcakes run. Therefore, I refuse to run. There's some mathematical principle at work, but I choose not to contemplate it.

This Sunday afternoon the running path winding through the coastal hill neighborhoods to the beach is full of people. I start slowly, my feet hitting the pavement with heavy *thwunks.*

At the end of the block, a pebble slides into the gap between the sneaker and my foot. I kick, but it falls into the bottom of my shoe and gouges the tender flesh of my arch. I screech to a stop and dig out the boulder. I despise Kennedy Green.

After another two blocks of uphill running, my lungs revolt. They refuse to pump air. A wave of nausea slams me. I slow to a walk and check my watch. Three minutes, and I haven't even made it to the quarter-mile mark. People who jog for fun are warped. People who run seven-minute miles are sadists.

The path curves down a long, sloping hill, and I welcome gravity to Team Rebel. Halfway down, my sneaker slides off the asphalt. My foot jams and twists. Pain shoots through my ankle.

Huffing, I lower myself until I'm sitting on the edge of the path. I take inventory: no blood, no protruding bones.

A shadow slices the sun. "What are you doing?" The voice is high-pitched and accusing. Cousin Pen.

I gulp in air, but it feels as if I'm sucking through a straw. "Run . . . ning."

"The cops after you?"

"Go"—huff—"to"—huff—"hell." Huff, huff.

"Seriously, are you okay?" Pen asks.

I gulp in another ten breaths, and my heart settles back in my chest. "I'm not dead."

"Let's see if you damaged anything." She squats in front of me and studies my foot. I brace myself, ready for her to yank at me and add to my misery. She slides her hand along my ankle and gives the bottom of my foot a push. "Does that hurt?"

"No."

She rotates my ankle. "And that?"

"Slight twinge."

"Let's see if you can stand." She holds out her hand.

I keep my butt on the ground. "What are you doing here?"

"Following you. I saw you leave the house. No stretching, no warm-up, your hair in your eyes. You do realize how stupid that is, right?"

"The backs of my calves, lungs, and right ankle are letting me know, loud and clear."

She jabs her hand at me again, and this time I take it. My right ankle twinges, but I can stand. Pen hands me a water bottle from a pack around her waist, and I shoot a stream of water into my mouth, rinse out my stupidity, and start hobbling back to the bungalow.

Pen falls into step beside me, walking as if she has a running shoe up her butt. Snob. But as the captain of the track team, she knows a lot about running.

"How long does it take you to run a mile?" I ask.

"That's random."

I shrug. Pen has no idea I'm completing the bucket list, and I can't wait for the day when I hand her the list, a check mark next to every item.

"My personal best is five fourteen."

"Please tell me that's five hours and fourteen minutes."

Pen doesn't dignify the comment with an answer.

When we get to the bungalow, I sink onto the bottom step of the porch and prop my ankle on the middle step. To my surprise, Pen settles her shoulder against the post. "First off," she says, "you're wearing the wrong shoes. You need something with better cushioning and traction. Before you start running, you need to warm up. At minimum, do leg stretches and back warm-ups. And for God's sake, Reb, get rid of those disgusting cigarettes. They are ruining your lungs."

Those "disgusting cigarettes" do such a good job of annoying those I wish to annoy, like Aunt Evelyn and my-lungs-are-in-perfect-shape Cousin Pen.

I take a long drink of water. "Why are you giving me advice?"

"Honestly?"

I jack my eyebrow at an angle.

"So you don't kill yourself and make my parents more upset." She seems almost wistful, not angry. "They never used to fight before you came into our lives."

10. Shake hands with an extraterrestrial

CHAPTER
ELEVEN

A SHOE BOX HAS MAGICALLY APPEARED AT THE foot of my bed. Inside sits a pair of pink running shoes, slightly used. They must be a pair of Cousin Pen's from her Amazon-growth days. In junior high she grew half a foot, while I added half an inch. She called me lima bean; I called her string bean.

The shoes have more tread than the pair I wore when I fell, and they'll fit tighter at the sides, keeping sharp rocks from impaling me. She must be serious about keeping me safe so I don't cause any more tension between her parents. I can't argue with her on that point. Most of Uncle Bob and Aunt Evelyn's shouting matches are about me.

During the past week, the bungalow has been oddly peaceful. To my surprise, Aunt Evelyn didn't gloat about getting me the Red Rocket trees, or, if she did, I was too busy doing bucket-list items to notice. Now Pen has gifted me with a pair of running shoes.

A week of wonders. Next thing we know, Tiberius will stop digging under the fence in search of sweets, and Macey and I will give each other manis and pedis.

For the next week I slip into Pen's old shoes, warm up, and run before school. My lungs burn, and muscles in my calves protest. Technically, I walk more than run, and I return gasping and covered in sweat, clocking in a dismal fourteen-minute mile. Aunt Evelyn watches me from the living room window. She probably thinks I'm on meth.

With Percy, I plant the Red Rocket trees in the school parking lot and start work on another bucket-list item: *Learn American Sign Language,* although I'll still need to work on the second part, *and volunteer to sign for the hearing impaired at church.* The tiny point of contention being, I don't have a church. I never felt at home in Uncle Bob and Aunt Evelyn's church. Too many rules about shoes.

At school I do my best to avoid random encounters with Nate, which isn't too hard since we swim in different oceans. I bypass the breezeway in front of Unit Five where he and the other jocks hang out. I steer clear of the baseball field where he works out most days after school. Biology is a bear. All week I listen to Nate *breathe.* It's crazy how I can distinguish his breathing from everyone else's. Maybe it's because we'd breathed as one. On the beach. In the cab of his father's truck. For his part, he doesn't mention anything about that moment in the truck and hasn't made any more attempts to get within a foot of the air I breathe this week.

So imagine my surprise on Friday afternoon when I get home and find Nate sitting on the porch, the right side of his hair a mess.

"Pen has track practice today," I say. "She'll be home after five."

"Reb—"

"And if you're selling, we don't need Scout-O-Rama tickets, our house number painted on the curb, or homemade enchiladas."

"We need to talk." He shifts his legs, making room for me on the step.

So many choices. I can leap over his legs and make a mad dash through the yard to the back door. Or I could dive over the fence and hang out with Tiberius.

"You were right," he says on a wobbly breath of air, which freaks me out because Nate is the type who doesn't wobble.

I sit and sigh. He toes the dried husk of a flower at the base of one of Aunt Evelyn's flowerpots.

"In this lifetime would be nice," I say.

He throws back his head and makes a sound, half laugh, half groan. "You're doing it again."

"Doing what?"

"Not giving a crap about trying to make me feel comfortable or making this any easier." He studies the porch step. "You're just being you." He crushes the husk, grinding it to dust. "You know who you are, and you refuse to be anything else. Honestly, on some days I wish I were you. I'd love to tell off my smart-ass friends. I'd love to tell my baseball coach I don't want to do another round of burners. I'd love to tell Mr. Phillips he has ugly ties and that it's cruel and unusual punishment to those of us in the front row."

I try to hold it back, but a laugh escapes.

"You don't care what others think. You don't compromise." Nate shifts one tennis shoe and then the other. "You're true to yourself and true to your word. Take this whole bucket-list thing. You said you'd complete Kennedy's list, and you're doing it." He shakes his head in amused disbelief. "And I have no doubt you'll do everything within your power to finish. You're true blue, and you were right that other night in the truck. For a moment I was worried about what my friends would think if they saw me with you. But sometime this week I stopped thinking." He doesn't say it, but I know the words hanging between us: *and started feeling.*

Nate's foot shifts and brushes against mine, the touch as light as the brush of the flower husk, but it hits me like a spring storm. I'm not denying what sparks between us, but it's scary. Nate likes perfect, and I am everything but perfect.

"You don't have to say anything," Nate says. "I just wanted you to know where I stand. If all we ever do is paint fake birds together, I'm fine. Well, not fine, but I can deal with it."

He lowers his head and studies his hands.

A silence settles between us.

I let out a Tiberius-like growl. "Do you always say the right thing?"

He contemplates me through the full black fans of his lashes, a slow smile curving his lips. "I try."

This can't work. I should run. But the truth is, I don't want to. I like the feel of Nate's foot against mine. I like the way he's looking at me. I like the fact that he's not filling the porch with noise. Perfect. Because he's Nate.

I rub invisible dust from the shark teeth on the strap of my messenger bag. "Do you know how to tango?"

"As in the dance?"

I nod.

"Bucket list?"

Another nod.

He stands and holds out his hand to me. "No. But I know someone who does."

At Nate's house, he plants me in the large sunroom where we painted bird decoys and goes to find his aunt, leaving me alone with the creepy statue in the corner, the one with angel wings and a sword.

"That's Saint Michael the Archangel." The youngest Bolivar stands in the doorway. "He protects us against the wickedness and snares of the devil."

"Marco! Rebel so does not want to talk about the snares of the devil." It's Little Miss Vogue. Today she wears a red felt hat tilted across her forehead and a gray sheath with red boots, very 1920s.

I nod but give Saint Michael my undivided attention.

The felt-hat girl sits on a chair next to me. "How do you get the blue color so bright?"

Saint Michael is grinding his foot into some guy's head but managing to look saintly.

"And how do you keep your hair so shiny and healthy look- ing? Are all those waves natural?"

Girl with Red Hat reaches out a hand, and I duck. "Go away."

"It's my house." She crosses her right leg over her left and swings a red boot. She stares and swings. Swings and stares.

"Exactly why are you watching me?" I ask.

The swinging stops. "You have panache." The little girl's eyes grow wide and shiny, like Macey's when she digs through peaches. "You have style and flair. People notice you."

"I don't give a damn about panache."

"Which makes it work even better. It's the juxtaposition of who you are on the outside with who you are on the inside. It totally works."

I can't believe I'm sitting next to a ten-year-old who uses

the word *juxtaposition*. And *panache*. "What's your name?"

"Carla Gabriella Maria Soltera Bolivar. Everyone calls me Gabby."

"Okay, Gabby. I'm going to be honest with you. With all your staring, you're bugging the shit out of me."

"You shouldn't swear."

I jump. The littlest Bolivar sits in a chair on my other side.

"And you shouldn't run around in your underwear," I say. Today's tightie whities are sprinkled with dump trucks.

He sticks out his tongue and runs away.

"People must stare at you all the time," Gabby says. "You're beautiful."

I'm not tall and leggy like Cousin Pen and the Cupcakes. I'm not elegant and put together like Aunt Evelyn. And I don't have that adventurous, windblown look my mother pulled off. Even with the blue streaks, I have average brown hair with average waves and average brown eyes.

Before I bemoan my less-than-average chest, Nate walks in with Tia Mina. She strokes her chin as she glides in a half circle around me. "You could do well at the tango. You short, but all legs. You have attitude. Passion."

"I have a pain-in-the-butt bucket list," I say under my breath.

Nate hides a chuckle behind his hand.

"Yes, I teach." She claps her hands and leaves the room, waving over her shoulder. "Take off shoes. I be back."

I kick off my flip-flops, and they make a happy, clacking

sound as they hit the tile floor. "I like this dance already."

Nate slips his hand along my back and guides me to the middle of the floor, his tennis shoes making soft, shuffling sounds, his palm firm and steady, as if there is nothing unusual about escorting girls with blue hair to tango lessons. A warped laugh builds in my chest, and I'm about to let it loose when Tia Mina walks back in, a pair of strappy black heels dangling from her fingers.

"For you," she says.

I wave off the offending creatures. "No, thank you."

"But Nate is so tall," Gabby says. "With the stilettos, you'll fit better in his arms."

"I can't walk in heels, let alone dance in them."

Gabby crosses her hands over her chest. "It's not a true tango without heels." Tia Mina nods.

Out of the corner of my eye, I catch Nate's arched eyebrow. "Fine. I'll wear the heels, but please note, I cannot be held liable for any bodily damage I cause to anyone in this room while in these shoes."

"I'll risk it." Nate's voice is a low thrum, his fingers warm against my back.

After I put on the heels, Tia Mina shows us how to create the frame. I rest my hand on Nate's rock-hard shoulder. I can see why he's one of the baseball team's superstars. Nate's hand settles at my waist. He must feel the butterflies stampeding in my midsection. Tia Mina joins our free hands, palm to palm, just like that moment in his dad's truck when we were surrounded only by darkness and the brush of each other's breath. My hand trembles, as if I'm going through nicotine withdrawal. Nate is steady, poised.

"Slow . . . slow . . . quick, quick . . . slow." Tia Mina claps her hands. "Got it?"

Nate nods. I don't. The movements are fast and jerky. My feet tangle, and I fall, my tailbone smacking the cold tile. "That would be slow . . . slow . . . quick, quick . . . crash," I say.

Nate helps me stand. We go through the movements again, Nate confident and encouraging. I step on his toes. I step on my toes. At one point I step on Gabby's toes.

"You don't go to many school dances, do you?" Gabby asks.

I ignore her. When I manage to make it across the floor without stumbling, Tia Mina announces we're ready to try it with music.

"And this," Gabby says. She thrusts a red bushy flower made of paper under my nose.

I wave off the monstrosity. "I am not going to hold a flower between my teeth."

"Don't be a dork, Rebel. It's for your hair." Gabby's nimble fingers slide through my hair as she pins the flower behind my ear.

"Perfect," Nate says as he takes me into his arms.

And for a single moment as I look up at him, I'm not a trapezoid, I'm not a misfit. I'm perfect.

Tia Mina puts on music, and Nate and I move about the room, sometimes gliding, sometimes falling. Each time, Nate scoops me off the ground with his big, strong hands. I watch his feet, focus on his fingers pressing into my back and guiding me. Nate sweats, a tiny pool at the collar of his T-shirt, but he's the type of guy who looks good in sweat. He lifts my arm and spins me. Then he pulls me to his chest, his heart thudding against mine. His breath fans my neck as we arch back. The room blurs around the edges.

"Not bad," he says, his lips against my ear.

No, not bad at all.

Tia Mina claps her hands. *"Basta!"*

"But I was getting the hang of it," I say.

She points to my high heels. "Feet need rest."

For the first time I notice the sharp pain on my heel where the strap digs into what feels like a blister. To say Nate has the power to distract me is an understatement.

I pull away from Nate and slow my breathing. "Check. Another bucket-list item complete."

Nate lowers his face toward me. "That was not about the bucket list."

So arrogant. So cocky. So true.

11. Buy a hundred Polly Pockets and send them to needy children in Africa

CHAPTER
TWELVE

"YOU HAVE CARBURETOR PROBLEM." A MAN IN NAVY overalls points to Nova, who is parked in front of the Bolivar house. The man has Nate's thick, dark hair, although sprinkled with gray at the temples, and Nate's dimples. He wears bandages on three knuckles of his right hand.

I switch off Nova's engine and hop off my scooter. "That's what Nate said."

Nate's dad unlocks the toolbox in the back of his old truck and takes out a short screwdriver. "My boy, he smart. Going to make money with head, not hands." Mr. Bolivar shows me his hands, the knuckles thick and covered with scabs, his fingertips cracked. He lifts the side case off my scooter and uses the screwdriver to turn a knob. "Natanel's going to get MBA, run big business, make big money."

I picture Nate in his dark suit the day of Kennedy's funeral. He looked good but not comfortable, tugging at his shirt as if it didn't fit right, jiggling his shoes as if they were too tight. I'm not sure if I can see him running a boardroom, but I know that whatever Nate chooses to do, he'll do it well. He can tutor and tango and flip my world upside down. And today he's going to install curved roof tiles on mudflats to serve as itty-bitty condos to protect baby sea swallows once they hatch, and I'm going to help.

"Now try it." Mr. Bolivar points the screwdriver at the ignition. I turn the key, and Nova hums. He pops the side case back on and climbs into his truck. I watch him pull away, taking note of how nice it feels to be on the other end of a random act of kindness.

Inside the house Gabby waits for me in the entryway. "Nate's at baseball practice. He called and told me to tell you his coach is making them all work another hour." She grabs my hand and pulls me to a sofa in the family room, giving me no time to concentrate on my disappointment. Stretching out on the back of the sofa, she pinches a lock of my hair between her fingers. "So how do you get it so blue?"

I tug the hair from her hand and try to glare, but she looks silly as her eyes cross in concentration. I laugh. "You're not going to leave me alone until I tell you, are you?"

She props her chin on her palm and gives me a cheesy grin. "Nope."

"You have patience, right? I mean, you're not one of these give-me-a-friggin'-ice-cream-cone-now-or-I'll-scream-my-head-off kids, are you?"

She slides off the back of the couch, her head dipping in a frantic nod.

"Where's your mom?"

"At work."

"Tia Mina?"

Gabby drags me to the kitchen, where Tia Mina is helping Nate the Younger pull a tray of flan from the oven. "May I kidnap Gabby?" I ask.

"Have her back by Monday morning, or the nuns at Our Lady of Sorrows Elementary School will cry."

Gabby squeals. "Where are we going?"

I lead her out of the kitchen. "You, Carla Gabriella Maria Soltera Bolivar, are going to experience a random act of kindness."

Outside in the Bolivars' driveway, Gabby climbs on the back of Nova, and I swear.

"What's wrong?" Gabby asks.

"I only have one helmet. We can't ride with one helmet." Her bottom lip quivers, and I want to kick myself. "I'm sorry, Gabby, but there are some rules that can't be broken. Everyone needs to wear a helmet."

Gabby jumps off the bike, and I'm worried she'll throw herself to the ground in a tantrum, but she runs into the house. Less than a minute later, she rushes out with a helmet, brandishing it like a trophy from the regional track-and-field meet. "It's Tia Mina's. She drives a sand rail."

"Of course the aunt who tangos also drives off-road vehicles," I say with an almost straight face.

"Tia Mina has done a lot of things since Tio Rogelio died. She rode an elephant, met the Pope, and swam with sharks. She says when she dies and goes to heaven, she wants to meet Saint Peter at the gates with no regrets."

Interesting. Another bucket list. I try to live fully and passionately in the moment without a bucket list, but maybe other people need one to get them started. Call me rebellious or daring, but when I die, I'll be a corpse with no regrets.

I put the helmet on Gabby and tighten the strap. I wonder if Kennedy had any regrets that day she drove off a cliff and crashed into the rocky sea. I imagine most people who die in accidents have regrets or unfinished business on Earth. Maybe that was the case with Kennedy. Maybe that's why I keep hearing her voice.

I pop my helmet onto my skull, knocking some sense into my head. Kennedy is not some kind of spirit caught between worlds, because the afterlife does not exist.

I help Gabby onto the seat and show her where to put her feet. As I climb on, she wraps her arms around me, her body snuggling against mine. A strange tremor shakes my torso. This is the first time someone has been on my scooter with me. Shaking off the startling realization, I turn the ignition and take off.

At the bungalow, I march Gabby through the living room, where Pen and a few Cupcakes are making *rah-rah* signs for an upcoming track meet. Pen drops her paintbrush and watches me with narrowed eyes.

"Chill, Pen. I only eat little children on days with full moons."

In the bathroom I point to the toilet. "Sit."

Gabby parks her squirming butt on the lid. I rummage through the cupboard under the sink and pull out a plastic basket. Gabby hugs her hands to her chest, and I freeze. If *happiness* had a picture in the dictionary, it would be Gabby's face. As I often do these days, I think of Kennedy. I wonder if this is why Kennedy chose to do so much good, to see these kinds of faces.

I clear the sudden thickness in my throat, reach into my hair basket, and take out a small bottle. "Here's the secret. No-frills store-brand dye from Bella's Discount Beauty Supply. Aisle three, bottom shelf. Electric Blue #1111. On sale days you can get it for eight ninety-nine."

"Eight ninety-nine."

I take out another bottle. "But before the hair dye you need to bleach out your natural color for the blue to take."

"Can you do it on my hair?" Gabby flips her thick fall of black, waist-length hair.

"No."

"Why not?"

"The nuns at Our Lady of Sorrows will kill me, if your parents don't get to me first."

"No, they won't. Nate likes you, and Mom and Dad like all of Nate's girlfriends."

I set the bottle of bleach on the counter and take out a tiny fan brush, plastic gloves, and foil. "Exactly how many has he had?"

"Girlfriends? Lots. Everyone loves Nate, but none of them have panache, like you." She squints her eyes and presses her lips together in her cheesy, butt-kissing grin. "So dye my hair. Pleeeeease."

"Not until your parents agree."

She scrunches her nose, and I can see the gears in her manipulative little brain whirring. "If they say yes, will you dye my hair blue for me?"

"Sure, but I want it in writing." I snap on the gloves. "In the meantime, I'll show you on a piece of my hair. That way you can do root touch-ups yourself after I do the initial dye job. I don't want you to end up with orange hair. Or worse."

She nods gravely. "Or worse."

I dig through the basket and find a narrow comb. "You want a straight, sharp section of hair. This gives the most dramatic flair."

"Dramatic flair."

I swallow a laugh. "Now for the bleach." I settle a foil beneath the hair strands.

"I think Nate and you should go to prom."

I uncap the bleach. "I think Nate and I should continue to paint rubber birds."

"I'm serious. He likes you. I mean *like* likes you."

"When applying the bleach, the secret is to fan out the hair. That way you'll get more even coverage."

"He looks at you. You know, in *that* way."

"It's a long and tedious process."

"And he—"

"Gabby?"

"What?"

"Shut up or you won't get blue hair."

She brings her thumb and forefinger to her closed mouth, twists, and pretends to throw away the key.

When Gabby and I get back to the house, Nate is sitting on the bench in the entryway, fresh from the shower, tying his tennis shoes. Drops of water pool on the tips of his hair and dampen the collar of his polo, while other water droplets slide along his collarbone, making his bronze skin glisten. Nate has his own brand of panache.

"Sorry I'm late." He stands and gives his head a wag. Droplets fly through the air, and I breathe in the clean smell of Nate. "We had the baseball practice from hell."

"A hell of your choosing," I say as we walk to the driveway.

"Thanks for the brutal honesty." Nate grins as he slides a long, muscled leg over Nova.

I freeze in the middle of the driveway. We're supposed to go to the mudflats to put in shelters for the baby chicks, a process that involves half-buried ceramic roof tiles, which should not require the need for any skin contact. "You want to take my scooter to the mudflats?"

"My dad took the truck."

I rock back on my heels.

"Is there something wrong?" Nate asks.

Not much. Just that we're about to get on a scooter, and you may very well wrap your arms around me and press your chest against my back.

What are you afraid of?

I rub the center of my forehead. *There are no such things as spirits. There are no such things as spirits.*

Nate reaches for my hand and pulls me toward him. Up close I can see the dampness spiking his lashes.

"Rebel, is there a problem?"

No lies.

The words brush the back of my neck in a whisper. I spin, searching for a blond perky ponytail. Of course I see nothing but Nate's empty driveway. Enough crazy. I grab Tia Mina's helmet and thrust it into Nate's stomach. "The problem is, you need a helmet."

At the mudflats, four other members of the 100 Club are waiting, and I'm thankful for them and the endangered sea swallows—anything to take my mind off the feel of Nate's legs around mine on the drive to the preserve. Nate directs club members to put up the chicken wire on the fence posts he'd set up last week. He explains that the fencing will keep out predators and human foot traffic. Then he takes me to a small mound of ceramic roof tiles.

"You and I will wedge these tiles into firmer sections of the mudflats." He thrusts a tile into a mound of banked earth. "Instant chick condos." Nate grins, his smile so wide and white, it takes my breath away. The lack of oxygen has apparently killed a few brain cells, because I can think of nothing to say. I grin and nod.

Lucky for me, I don't have to say much over the next four hours as construction on the nesting site continues. All afternoon Nate and I dig and construct and clear weeds. From one of the other club members I learn that Nate's spent more than a hundred hours on the site. A guy like Nate cares. He cares about endangered birds. He cares about good grades, the Del Rey School baseball team, his family, and me.

Me. Nate cares about me. A strange wave of something light and electric washes over me, and I steady myself on my shovel.

After the last ceramic tile is in place, I rinse my shovel in a shallow inlet and take it to Bronson's Mustang. Nate stands at the trunk—shirtless—loading the supplies. A small gold cross dangles from a chain around his neck. Mud streaks his arms and legs, and sweat dampens the waist of his sporto shorts, a look that totally beats his funeral suit. I almost drop my shovel before I can slip it into the trunk of Bronson's car.

"You need a ride, Nate-O?" Bronson asks as the other three club members climb into the sports car. He says nothing to me. "We can make room for you."

"Nope." Nate grabs his shirt from a fence post. "Reb and I have one other thing to do."

Bronson scans me from head to toe, and I feel every bit of cracked mud and dried sweat. Unlike Nate, I don't rock the sweaty-construction-worker look. I pick a line of mud from my fingernail and blow Bronson a kiss.

After they drive off, Nate grabs my hand and takes me out of the mudflats and along the boardwalk. His pace is unhurried, his sun-bronzed face relaxed. He loves it out here. Like me. When I first arrived in Tierra del Rey after Mom's death, I spent hours at the beach. Aunt Evelyn thought I was trying to avoid the family, and she even took me to a counselor, who finally helped me convince her that I simply love the sand and water and wide-open spaces.

At the end of the boardwalk, Nate pulls me into a boat rental shop managed by one of his friends. When he sees us, the friend drags out a long, narrow boat.

"Kayaking?" I ask. "We're going kayaking?"

"Better than kayaking." Nate slides the boat along the sand

toward the ocean, and I remember another item from the "fun" section of Kennedy's bucket list:

Ride in a gondola in Venice, Italy, with the love of my life.

I dig my toes into the cool sand. Nate Bolivar is certainly not the love of my life, and I'm not headed to Italy, but the kayak is a long, skinny boat, much like a gondola. It could work.

"Reb, you good to go?"

I almost laugh out loud at the goodness washing over me like sunshine. It's good, all good.

Nate and I carry the kayak to the swash zone, where we both rinse off mud and sweat. He holds the kayak steady as I climb into the backseat, and soon we're paddling through the harbor. Mr. Athlete's strokes are fast and smooth, and I watch the bunch and stretch of his arm and back muscles. Soon I fall into a nice rhythm with him.

We glide past a kelp bed, and Nate shifts his body and points to a harbor seal sunbathing with her cub. The sun glints off his hair, painting it with streaks of gold. If Bella's Discount Beauty Supply could bottle that color, they'd make a million. "Now ready to see something that'll take your breath away?"

You're doing fine, thank you very much.

We paddle past the mudflats to a rocky cliff. Dozens of pelicans nest on the jagged face, most squawking as we draw near. Nate taps my leg and points to the shallows, where a pair of narrow, shadowy figures glide. "Leopard sharks," he says quietly but keeps paddling.

The cliff face grows closer, blocking out the sun. My hands tighten around the paddle bar. "Hey, we're going to cr—"

Nate angles the kayak and sends us into a fissure in the cliff, the opening so narrow, I can reach out with both arms and touch the sides. The air cools and darkens. I slip off my sunglasses. The sea is a black mirror. Nate continues to paddle, steering us through a twisting passage. The air grows heavy, dank, and the ceiling slopes. Nate's hair brushes the top of the cave, and the walls close in on us so tightly, we can't use our paddles. Nate pushes off the sides of the cave with his hands.

We round one more bend and burst into a sea of brilliant light. Above us stretches blue sky. The boat glides along on a pane of sparkling blue glass. Fish, neon blue and yellow and green, play beneath the glassy water. I breathe deeply.

Nate tilts back in his kayak seat and crosses his arms over his chest as if he's watching a movie. "I call it God's Masterpiece."

I'm too busy marveling at the light-filled cavern and bright blue water to argue the ludicrous name. "I've lived here six years and come to the beach almost every day but never knew this existed."

"We're not supposed to be in the sea caves without a licensed guide. It can get pretty dangerous out here with the tides, but no worries, we have a good hour before the water level starts to shift."

I'm not worried. Nate has everything under control.

A school of long, silvery fish dart under the kayak. A trio of sunny orange fish tumbles by like a bowl of spilled fruit. Nate swipes the water with his paddle, and we glide toward a rocky shelf. On it sits a constellation of sea creatures. Starfish and flowerlike anemones, hundreds of them. "I've never seen anything like this," I say on a rush of air. "I wish I had paint and paper."

"How about a photo?" Nate's fingers brush against mine as he holds out his phone, and I can't help but remember the warmth of our intertwined hands and his words. *I like you, Rebel.* Heat rushes along my neck. Nate presses the phone into my hand, but my fingers fumble. The phone tumbles toward the water.

Nate lunges across me and rescues the phone before it hits the water. On his way back to his seat, he pauses for a half second. His head dips, and he brushes his lips across mine. A single kiss, as swift and fleeting as the rainbow of fish below.

So many colors in the water. Colors in my head. Bright and silvery and flashing. A different shade of confetti light.

I open my eyes. Nate sits in his seat, his eyes looking everywhere but at me, his hand worrying the side of his hair, now ruffled. "I shouldn't have done that." He fumbles with the paddle. "I told myself I wasn't going to do that. I'm sorry."

I dig my paddle into the pebbly bottom of the sea cave, steadying the rocking kayak. I wait until he finally looks at me. "I'm not."

12. Have a campout in the Louvre
and make s'mores

CHAPTER
THIRTEEN

"WHAT'S YOUR TIME?" PEN ASKS FROM HER PERCH on the top step of the bungalow's front porch. Her backpack and gym bag sit at her feet.

I press my palms against the small of my back and walk up the brick path. I breathe deeply, forcing the cool, early-morning air into my lungs. "Nine. Forty. Two." My hair hangs damp against my neck, and there's an ache in my chest. My body feels spent but good, a nice buzz tingling along my limbs. I've been running every morning for two weeks, pushing myself to go farther and faster each time, and I've smoked only six cigarettes in twelve days. Ms. Lungren would be proud of this lifestyle change.

Pen plucks at the paper crane dangling from the zipper pull of her backpack. If she glanced at me, I wonder if she could see the other change—if she could tell that I'd kissed Nate. Nate's kiss had warmed me to the tips of my blue hair. It made me forget about failing math grades and a dead girl's bucket list. It felt right.

A yellow VW Bug with daisy hubcaps pulls up in front of the house. The driver, a Cupcake, honks. Pen straightens the crane's wings. "So here's the deal." She unfolds and refolds the crane's tail and doesn't say anything else.

I lift my hair, letting the breeze fan my neck. "Sometime this decade would be nice."

Pen stands and heaves her backpack, crane and all, onto her shoulder. "With Kennedy gone, we're down a member on the track team. We have two more meets and regionals. After doing the math, it's clear that if we want to go into regionals as top seed"—she sighs and finally looks at me—"we need another body."

The post-run buzz bubbling through my veins ices. "Pen, I'm not a runner, and I'm certainly not a team player. Can you say 'soccer'?"

Aunt Evelyn made me play soccer the first year I was here to help me "make lifelong friends and get physically fit." I joined Penelope's club team of little soccer superstars who'd been playing since being drop-kicked from the womb. At first I loved soccer. I loved running and booting the ball. I loved how the lead scorer performed a funky little dance every time she made a goal, and I couldn't wait to show everyone my funky little dance. But there were so many rules and flags and whistles that no one bothered to explain, and I never got to perform my happy I-made-a-goal dance, not even when I kicked the ball through the posts for my first and only point. Unfortunately, I'd kicked the ball into the other team's goal. Coach pulled me from the game, and my teammates snickered and started calling me Wrong-Way Reb. Cousin Pen was mortified.

"Track-and-field isn't like soccer," Pen says. "In soccer, if you score more goals, you win. In track-and-field, it's a numbers game. We need to participate in X number of events with Y number of people and earn Z number of points."

"You know I suck at math, right? Plus, there's the little fact that I'm not a good runner."

"I know that. We don't need someone to make the final rounds. We just need another body to replace Kennedy Green so we can max out all of the events. All we need for you to do is show up." She fiddles with the strap of her backpack. The crane twitches, as if it's having an epileptic fit.

I savor the moment. Squirm, Pen, squirm, for you are not in charge. She's not showing me around *her* school, introducing me to *her* friends, or ordering me when to fold my hands in *her* church. She's not telling me which dresser drawers to use or lecturing me on how the family opens Christmas presents. With the toe of one running shoe, I push on the heel of the other and kick. Pink leather flies across the porch, and I wiggle my toes. For the first time in her life, Cousin Pen needs me.

We should probably help her.

My toes dig into the heel of my other shoe. *This is none of your business, Kennedy.*

You're pushing me away again.

I slide off the shoe and lob it across the porch, wishing I could do the same thing with Kennedy Green, but she's wormed her way into my head. I hear her daily, which makes sense, given that I haven't missed a daily random act of kindness. With a growl, I yank off my socks. Joining the track team would qualify as a random act of kindness. Hell, it would be the extreme edition of random acts of kindness. Doing a favor for Pen. Running with the Cupcakes. Wearing the dorky little sporto outfit. I shiver.

The Cupcake in the driveway honks again.

Pen stops fiddling with her backpack, and the crane stills. In her stillness, she's nothing like the shouting, stabbing, quivering girl who accused me of causing damage and destruction to everything I touched. During the past week, she scooped me off the pavement and gave me pink shoes. There'd been peace in the bungalow. Plus, she had to go and mention Kennedy Green.

"Just show up?" I look at my shoe leaning against the screen door, as if it's trying to escape this crazy conversation.

"Just. Show. Up."

I slip into biology as the tardy bell rings and hurry to my desk.

"That's two weeks of perfect attendance, Ms. Blue." Mr. Phillips makes a note in his attendance book. "Your newfound punctuality and focus continue to delight and amaze."

"I agree," Nate says, dimples like the Grand Canyon.

My knee knocks the lab stool, and I steady it before it crashes to the ground. I'm already off-balance because of Pen's invitation to join the school's track team, but that dimple sends me reeling. "Hey."

Before either of us can say anything, Mr. Phillips continues our unit on animal behaviors. Today he talks about ants who build bridges with their bodies. "Connections, students. These ants can build bridges over entire rivers with the right connections."

Nate slides his notebook toward me, a single word written in the margin of the page. *Lunch?*

It's funny how one little word can mean so much. Nate wants to eat lunch with me at school. In front of everyone. What a change from that moment in his father's truck.

So much has changed. Penelope asked me to join the track team, and I agreed. Even Mr. Phillips's tie doesn't appear atrocious today. If I squint, I see a field of tulips dotting the silk around his neck.

I'm glad Nate wants to eat lunch with me, but I can't.

Not today, I write in the margin of my notebook.

Why?

Pies.

?

Long story.

Meet after school?

Can't.

?

Track practice.

Nate drops his pen, and I laugh out loud at the stunned expression on his face. Mr. Phillips taps my desk with his pointer. "Pay attention, Rebecca."

"I can't do it." Macey jams her hands into her hoodie pocket and turns away from the pies sitting on the FACS kitchen counter.

"You have to." I grab two pies and motion toward the other two with my chin. "Lungren already set up the signs, and people are expecting us."

"Since when do you care about other people's expectations?" Macey's tone is unusually harsh and loud.

"This isn't about me, Macey. It's about you and pies and kicking ass at the Great American Bake-Off." I give her one of Gabby's cheesy grins. "Now get the pies. Lungren reserved two tables in the front of the cafeteria. Should be the perfect place for taste tests."

Macey leans her butt against the cupboard. I'm about to

nudge her with my elbow when I hear The Voice, aimed not at me, but Macey.

What are you afraid of?

My pies wobble, and I steady them. *Quiet, Kennedy. You have no idea what's going on.*

Macey's shoulders hunch, as if she's trying to disappear into herself.

I set down the pies. "What's wrong, Macey?"

She runs her toe along a glob of dried piecrust on the floor. "There are going to be a lot of people in there."

"So?"

"They'll be staring at me."

"No, they'll be staring at the pies." I watch the sugared blueberries sparkle in the bright light streaming through the FACS classroom window. "Really, Macey, these look amazing." She's been making pies for three weeks, trying different crusts and fillings and toppings, and we're going to bring the top four to the school cafeteria for a taste test to determine the best of the best. At least, that's my brilliant idea.

"I'm not like you, Rebel. You like standing out. You shine when you're in the spotlight." Macey rotates her wrists, the hoodie fabric bunching about her hands. "I turn into a giant slug."

We all need friends.

Okay, I'll give you this one, Kennedy.

Macey may not be signing my yearbook with *x*s and *o*s, but sometime over the past few weeks, sometime between tandem riding and shopping for peaches, she's become more than a detention comrade and friend-of-convenience, and for some reason I don't know but accept, pies are important to her. "You don't have to shine, Macey. You don't even have to talk."

She looks skeptically at me through wisps of ethereal blond hair.

"Like you said, I have no problem standing out. I'll serve pie and ask the questions. You can sit in the corner and take notes. Now grab the pies, and let's get to the cafeteria."

Macey stares at her feet.

"Come on, Mace. If I can spend a month on the track team, you can spend an hour in the cafeteria."

Her face the color of ash, Macey grabs the pies and follows me out of the FACS classroom.

I have not set foot in the Del Rey School cafeteria since December, when I'd been on one of Lungren's detention assignments. Along with three other detention sods, I power-washed crud, formerly known as cafeteria food, from the walls.

Today the lunchroom is aglow with sharp fluorescent light and heavy with the smell of too many bodies and marinara sauce. I spot Pen and the Cupcakes at one of the center tables. Nate and some of his sporto pals sit nearby. As Macey and I make our trek along the front wall, he sees me and waves. It's another public declaration.

Hey, world! Nate of Great Hair has a thing for Rebel Blue.

I wave back.

We find the table in the corner where Lungren has posted a large sign that reads *Pie Tasting Today*. Macey and I place the pies at one end of the table. She takes out napkins, plastic serving spoons, and a clipboard. Before long, a dozen people line up at the other end of the table. Macey turns, as if she's going to bolt, and I grab the back of her hoodie, holding her in place. She finally gives her hoodie sleeves a tug and hands me a spoon. "Everyone gets a bite-size piece. Be sure to include the filling and the crust."

"No worries," I say, stealing Nate's favorite phrase.

For twenty minutes I serve pie and ask questions while Macey takes notes. The whole thing goes smoothly, like a well-oiled tandem bike, until a girl with crinkly black hair arrives. Macey's face goes from sickly gray to deathly white.

"Oh, good, you made it, Clementine!" Lungren rushes back to the pie-tasting table. "I'm so excited you decided to report about Macey's Great American Bake-Off aspirations. It's such a compelling human-interest story." Lungren points to the crinkly-haired girl. "This is Clementine Radmore, the student journalist I told you about. She's the general manager of KDRS, the school radio station. You know about them, right?"

Even I know about the school radio station. Last year some half-brain got upset about one of the station's talk shows and torched the building, but the police found him, and he's doing community-service hours that would get him a few years' worth of centurion status in the 100 Club. The station now streams on the Internet, and I tune in on Sundays for its indie music programs with DJ Taysom.

Macey clutches her clipboard to her chest.

The radio reporter pulls out a digital recorder and holds it to her chin. "How many kinds of pie have you baked to date?"

"Er . . . um . . . thirty," Macey says in a barely-there voice.

"And you've narrowed down your Great American Bake-Off entries to how many kinds?"

Macey holds up four fingers.

The reporter's nostrils flare like a dragon's, but Macey says nothing. She looks as if she wants to duck under a lunch table.

"All the finalists are made with peaches," I say. "Why don't you tell Clementine about the peaches?"

"Peaches," Macey repeats. She tilts her head toward the table. "I have peaches and cream with a shortbread crust and one with a graham-cracker crust and then another with a buttermilk crust. I also have three different toppings, including one with blueberries." As she speaks, I point to the pies, like one of those models on a game show. Macey's face has lost some of its deer-in-the-headlights look. "Right now I'm using frozen peaches."

"Why?"

"The fresh ones aren't ripe."

The radio reporter asks a few more questions, which Macey answers with complete sentences before the reporter closes off with, "This is Clementine Radmore reporting for KDRS 88.8, The Edge."

After the reporter leaves, Macey hugs the clipboard to her chest and nods her head at the empty pie plates, and I can hear her think, *Well done, little pies, well done.* If I can talk to a dead girl, Macey can certainly talk to her pies. After we clean the pie table, I walk with Macey to the cafeteria door, and Nate waves me over.

"I can clean up," Macey says. "There's not much, and we have plenty of time until the bell rings."

Which means I have plenty of time to sit with Nate, who sits in his little corner of the cafeteria universe with the people he calls friends. I dig my toes into my flip-flops. This is what I asked for yesterday in the sea cave when I told him I didn't regret the kiss. I like being with Nate. My world feels right with Nate. And I don't care who knows it.

I slide onto the seat next to him at a lunch table populated by heavenly bodies, the Del Rey School's superstars. Across from me is the football player Pen dated all winter. He gives me a strange look, and I blow him a kiss. The Cupcake who went to homecoming last year with Nate stares at me with her mouth agape. I wave. Cousin Pen sits two tables down, and, despite the distance, I hear her groan.

"How were the pies?" Nate asks.

"Peaches with sugared blueberries is the early favorite."

"How about some flan? My brother Mateo said he wanted

you to try his raspberry sauce." Nate opens a small bowl and hands me a spoon. I take a bite of the puddinglike dessert and let it slide along my tongue. Sweet.

Voices rumble around me. The people to my right talk of division rankings for the track team, and to my left a few others talk about elections for next year's student body council. Nate, of course, is thinking about running for school president. His shoulder nudges mine. It's as hard as marble but warm and has that nice, clean Nate smell. "What do you think, Reb?"

"I think being school president sounds like a boatload of work."

"But it will look good on college apps."

"And you'll do a good job," one of the Cupcakes says.

"But do you have time?" I ask. Nate could join a support group for High School Students Who Do Too Much.

"I'll have time if I choose to make time," Nate says.

"Exactly. It all comes down to choices. You have limits on your time, and you have to ask yourself if being class president—running meetings, organizing a trip to Disneyland, and listening to people argue about the senior gift—is really how you want to spend it."

"There could be worse ways to spend time than beefing up on leadership skills and helping others."

"Forget about *others* for a moment." I point my spoon at the center of Nate's chest. "If you knew you'd die in a year, would you really run for class president?"

Nate's gaze grows thoughtful. "No, I guess I wouldn't."

"Because . . ." At this section of the lunch table, the chatter dies.

"Because I'd be doing other things, things that are more important and meaningful to me."

I smile around another bite of flan. "Exactly."

"But last time I checked," says the girl who went to homecoming last year with Nate, "Nate's heart was very much beating."

The guy on his right pops him on the shoulder. "You're not going all cancer on us, are you, Nate-O?"

Nate shakes his head, and his former homecoming date holds up both hands. "Do we really need to talk about death and cancer while we're eating?" She looks at me and wrinkles her nose. "This really does seem inappropriate."

I open my mouth and *choose* to cram in another bite of flan. It's good. Probably made with fresh raspberries.

The guy next to Nate drags him into a conversation about this week's baseball game, while the girl on my right points a celery stick at the messenger bag hanging across my chest. "That's such an interesting . . . uh . . . fashion accessory. Where'd you get it? The bottom of the sea?"

Time for another choice. I can sling snark as usual, but these are Nate's friends, and, contrary to what Cousin Pen thinks, I'm not a bulldozer. I don't want to cause damage and leave destruction in my wake. "It was my mother's. She bought it years ago at a thrift store and used it to hold her camera and lenses. It's been all over the world."

"A thrift store? Do you get your clothes there, too?" Nate's former homecoming date pinches her lips into a little O. "Like those undershirts. Um, nice stuff."

"Yeah, actually. They come from a thrift store off Calle Bonita."

The first girl shudders. "I don't think I'd be too comfortable with other people's used underwear."

I take another bite of flan, even though I want to take a bite out of Bitchy and Bitchier. All of a sudden I'm back in middle school. I remember eating lunch with a group of fellow unpopulars in the seventh grade—I'd already been ostracized by Cousin Pen and the in-crowd by that time—when one of my friends asked if the new shirt she was wearing made her look fat. It was one of those trendy, scrunchy shirts that hugged every inch of flesh. The shirt bit into her arms and didn't cover the last roll of pudge of her stomach, even though she kept tugging the hem. Every girl at our table oohed and aahed, offering various versions of "No, it looks fantastic!" I was so confused, I stopped eating. Girls at other lunch tables were snickering and pointing at my friend, who looked not just overweight, but uncomfortable. When my friend asked, "Honestly, Rebel, does this make me look fat?" I simply said, "Yes." I spent the rest of the year eating alone in the school courtyard because I didn't understand the language of girls. Now I do, or at least bits and pieces. Nate's friends at the lunch table want to irritate me, to set me off, to prove to Nate that I don't belong.

Morons. I take a bite of flan, keep my mouth shut, and scoot closer to Nate.

13. Swim in bioluminescent algae

CHAPTER
FOURTEEN

THE DEL REY TRACK TEAM PRACTICE JERSEY IS orange and yellow and clashes with my hair. Nate's sister, Gabby, would not be impressed, and she'd have a fit over the shorts, two funky polyester tubes hanging awkwardly around my legs. The shorts are only moderately heinous on the other track team members with their buff legs and golden tans.

I jog to the center of the field, where the championship Del Rey School women's track-and-field team gathers in a circle and stares at me. I am a curiosity, a standout. Normally I'd take pleasure in that, but this afternoon I feel oddly naked. Maybe it's because I had to leave my shark-teeth bag in my gym locker.

Pen jogs over, her eyebrows raised. I need a cigarette.

Unfortunately, they're with the shark teeth. "You made it," Pen says.

"Just show up?"

"Yeah, just show up." Pen's eagle eyes roam over me. "Here, you'll need this." She slips a ponytail holder from around her wrist. I picture Kennedy's ponytail, bouncing as she darted to her car in the parking lot after detention. The image is so clear, so bright, along with the realization that *she* should be here on this track with these people, not me.

People are exactly where they need to be when they need to be there.

A breeze rushes by me, heavy with sunshine and citrus.

I spin in a circle, a crazy part of me searching for a bobbing ponytail.

Pen waves a hand in my face. "Earth to Reb." My cousin forces the ponytail holder into my clenched fist. "Use this to keep your hair out of your face so you don't trip and hurt yourself. I swear, sometimes you're clueless."

My hand trembles as I tie back my hair with the ponytail holder, and I remind myself that Kennedy is dead. She is not here, and I am here because I made the *choice* to be here.

Captain Pen leads the group through a series of stretches that involve my nose getting intimate with my kneecap way too many times. After the warm-up, one of the assistant coaches announces she's going to put me "through the events" to learn my various base times. I run sprints, and with a perplexed frown she records my times. Her disposition remains far from sunny as we head to the field, where I perform dismally on the long jump and high jump. At the throwing circle, I drop a shot-put on her toe and bang myself in the head with a discus. The coach doesn't let me near the javelin.

"Let's try the hurdles," she says. "You're pretty short, but we're down a leaper." That would be Kennedy. "You're not jumping over the hurdle so much as using your forward momentum to glide over the bar. You want your lead leg at a ninety-degree angle as you approach the hurdle, driving with the knee, not the toe. On your trail leg, you want your calf parallel with the bar. Got it?"

I get that this sounds like math. At the first hurdle, I have no problem because I sprint around it. A team member standing near the bench folding towels giggles. The assistant coach does not. When I finally get the nerve to leap over the hurdle, my feet tangle in the bar, and I fall, scraping my knee along the rough track surface.

"I think we've had enough today," the coach says. "Why don't you get the trainer to fix that, and you can call it quits?"

"I'd love to."

The girl folding towels introduces herself as Liia, the team's trainer. She directs me to a bench and pulls out a first-aid kit. "Pretty ugly."

"Are you referring to my knee or my future on the Del Rey School's track-and-field team?"

With a chuckle, she cleans the dirt and gravel from my skin. As she pulls a bandage from the first-aid kit, I notice a bag of cut-up oranges on her supply table, and for the first time since my pink running shoes landed on the track, I smile. This is the source of the citrus smell, not the spirit of Kennedy Green.

With the bandage in place, I head for the locker room to get my things. I want nothing more than to crawl into my attic and watch the light bounce off jars of sea glass and maybe think about Nate. As I make my way past the baseball practice field, Nate jogs over to the chain-link fence surrounding the field.

"How'd it go?" Nate asks.

"There was blood."

He rests his forearms on the top of the fence and widens his stance, so we're eye level. "It'll get easier, Reb. The first few days of any workout are always the toughest. Coaches need to know where you're at physically and mentally."

"It's not a good place, Nate, so not a good place."

Nate kneads my shoulders. "Bucket list?"

"Do you need to ask?"

In addition to a megawatt smile that makes me forget about skinned knees and mean girls, today Nate wears baseball pants, stained at the knees and calves, and a DRS varsity baseball shirt.

"Nate!" Some guy near the batting cage waves. "In the box! You're up!"

His fingers do marvelous things to the muscles along my

shoulders. "You should go," I say, which is clearly not the same as *I want you to go*.

His hands slide to the back of my neck, and the magic continues. "Yeah," he says, sighing. "College scouts are coming to next week's game."

"And you will duly impress?" Because that's what Nate does, impresses the world, me included.

"That's The Plan."

"The Plan?" I angle my head and look up at him out of the corner of my eye. "Sounds rather impressive."

"Sixteen years in the making. I'll be the first in my family to go to college."

Nate's dad said something about Nate using his head, not his hands, to make a living. "It's important to your dad, isn't it?"

Nate laughs. "Just a little. He bought a file cabinet my freshman year so I could organize all my college planning stuff. This year he spent his Christmas bonus taking me on a college visit to Stanford."

It must be nice to have so much family support. When I told the residents of the bungalow that I wanted to go to art school, Penelope laughed, practical Uncle Bob suggested I get a teaching degree, and Aunt Evelyn grew uncharacteristically silent.

"Nate!" The guy at the batting cage swings his arm in an angry arc. "Get in gear!"

"Gotta go before Coach has a coronary." Nate leans against the fence, the chain-link groaning, and pulls me toward him. He brushes a kiss on my lips, feathery soft, sweetly cool. The pains in my knee and neck disappear.

Someone in the dugout lets out a catcall. Nate pulls away and heads for the batting cage while I head for the locker room and another bucket-list item.

The list. It's all about the list, and when I'm done with Kennedy's list, when I'm no longer living out her dreams and desires, she'll be gone, and I'll be back to myself, to my old life, which means no more track team, no more ugly turtles, no more skinned knees.

In the locker room, I shower and change and wonder if the new version of my old life will include Nate. Once I'm no longer channeling do-gooder Kennedy, he may no longer want to rub the tension from my neck and warm me to the tips of my toes. He may realize I'm not the girl for him.

I shove my sporto stuff into my messenger bag and hurry out of the locker room. I don't have time to worry about Nate. The bucket list beckons. I check the time and start to jog as fast as my wounded knee will allow. I need to be at the mall in twenty minutes, so I take a shortcut under the stadium bleachers.

"Hey, Reb!" One of the guys from the baseball team runs toward me. "You dropped something." Afternoon light slants through the bleachers, striping everything, including the pink tennis shoe dangling from his fingertips.

I toss the shoe into my bag. "Thanks."

"Is that all I get?" He hooks a hairy knuckle around the strap of my bag. "I heard you're giving Nate a little more than thanks."

I unhook his finger. "I need to go."

He edges closer, his entire body striped with shadow. "Come on, Reb, give a little."

"Give me a break, ass-wipe." I sling my bag across my chest and hurry through the striped light.

He jumps in front of me and walks backward. "We both know a guy like Nate is with you for one reason." He runs a Neanderthal knuckle along my arm. "How about—"

I swat away his hand and duck under his armpit, gagging on the putrid stench.

"I get it. A girl like you likes it a little rough." He grabs both of my shoulders, his hands chilling manacles, and jerks me back toward him.

Something cold and sharp twists in my stomach as he grins, one hairy hand groping my tank. The striped shadows deepen, sending slashes of black across his face.

I bend my knee, as if I'm about to bolt over a hurdle, and kick. He grunts and doubles over. My heart thundering against the shark teeth, I lean over his folded body and whisper in his ear, "A girl like me isn't afraid to kick a guy like you in the balls."

I grab a handful of napkins from The Pretzel Man cart in the Del Rey Fashion Mall food court and rub my arm, trying to wipe off Neanderthal Boy's touch. I rub harder, but there's no heat. My skin is cold, my blood colder.

With a hard toss, I throw the napkins into the trash and search for a man in a *Star Wars* T-shirt. From my vantage point in front of the pretzel cart, I spot one guy in a *Star Trek* T-shirt and two *Doctor Who*s. The guy in the *Star Trek* T-shirt stands on his chair.

"*Star Trek*?" I say. "The instructions in the e-mail said he'd be wearing a *Star Wars* T-shirt."

Next to me a lady hands each of the toddlers in a double stroller a soft pretzel stick and stands. "Mine, too. Maybe he got tired of doing laundry. I could see that. I'm so tired of laundry." Her voice is low and raspy, like the gasp of air from a deflating balloon. "Everyone told me to use disposable diapers: my sisters, the women in my mom's group, my husband, but I wanted to do things right, for the twins, for the environment. You know?" She stands close to me, and our shoulders touch.

"Uh . . . sure."

"But there are some days when I can't stand it. The smell of bleach. The snowy white piles." Her head spins in a dizzy circle. "They're like mountains."

"Snow-covered mountains," I say, my head spinning in tandem with hers.

She closes her eyes and tilts her head back as if her neck can no longer support the weight of her thoughts. "Some days the diaper mountains are too steep to climb."

"So let them go without diapers," I say. "My mom did."

The woman's eyes burst open. "Really?"

"She hated housework." Which is one of the reasons we never had a house.

One of the toddlers fusses, and the woman hands him the entire carton of pretzel sticks. "And you survived."

I laugh. "Yeah, I did."

The woman squeezes my hand. "I can't wait. Are you ready?"

For another bucket-list item: *Participate in a flash mob*. Um, yeah, I can wait, especially with my bandaged knee, which still throbs from my intimate encounter with the track hurdle. And I'm still feeling chilled from the jerk groping me under the bleachers, because for half a heartbeat, I was afraid he was going to take something I'd chosen not to freely give. For a moment I was powerless.

The overcrowded food court buzzes with voices. Light pours in from the skylights over the central atrium, and all around us food pops and sizzles and steams. This place should be hot. Even in my tank, I should be sweating, but I can't shake the cold.

Mr. *Star Trek* raises his arm.

"Time to get into position." The woman with diaper issues giggles and squeezes my hand. "This is so exciting."

People pour into the food court like ants, spilling out of shops and sliding away from tables. I picture Mr. Phillips's ants from biology, the ones that build bridges with their bodies, locked together, a mass of tiny creatures capable of big feats. Laundry

Mom and I stand near the stroller as people gather around us. A guy my age with a shaved head and a gray-haired woman with practical shoes stand in front of us.

Mr. *Star Trek* whistles. The bodies spread out. Laundry Mom gives my hand another squeeze.

"Bow to your partner!" Mr. *Star Trek* calls out. "Now bow to your corner!"

Around us shoppers stop eating. People stop on the stairs. The girl at the pretzel cart stops twisting pretzel dough. A fiddler standing in the middle of the food court starts swinging his bow.

"Circle round, now circle round!" Mr. *Star Trek* calls.

The ants circle, and I crash into the old lady, a dagger of pain piercing my knee.

"You're circling the wrong way, dear," she says as she pats my shoulder. "Circle right, circle right."

Laundry Mom and I hold hands and promenade. "I don't hate my life," she says over the fiddle music. "And I don't hate the twins. I hate laundry, and only some of the time." Her cheeks are as rosy as the toddlers sitting in the stroller, clapping along with the song.

At last Mr. *Star Trek* whistles again, and the music stops. Everyone drops hands and heads back to their tables and shopping.

"Is that the coolest thing or what?" Laundry Mom squeezes my hand. "I've never participated in a flash mob before. I mean, we're total strangers one minute, then we're connected." The tired lines around her eyes smooth out. "And we'll probably never see each other again." She grabs both of my hands and brings them to her chest. "What's your name?"

"Rebecca. Rebecca Blue."

"Well, Rebecca, I'm Samantha Grayson, and I'm glad we were here. Together. At this moment." After one more squeeze, she grabs the stroller and wheels away, her ponytail bobbing.

That's when I realize that the chill that had settled in under the bleachers is gone. Warmth floods my arm.

You were here for me when I needed you, and I'm here for you.

14. Plant a secret garden

CHAPTER
FIFTEEN

THE NEXT MORNING I LIMP TO PERCY'S OFFICE, A large maintenance supply closet near Unit One. He stands at his workbench, where an easel with a single broken leg lies like an amputee on an operating table. As usual, his eye twitches as he works.

I lean my hip against his workbench, and my messenger bag falls to the ground with a heavy *clunk*. Today I need a place far away from crowds and track hurdles and flash mobs. Today I need to turn off the world, because I need to think.

For weeks Kennedy has been in my head, talking about fate and destiny, and I've been arguing that the choices I make control me. They make me who I am and determine my future.

But last night at the flash mob, I had a chance encounter with Samantha Grayson, who was exactly where I needed her when I needed her, and vice versa. I threw a life preserver at a mother drowning in laundry, and she warmed my hands. Kennedy would have said that some higher being or unseen force had brought us together.

I slide along the side of the workbench and sit on a five-gallon bucket of something called Sudsy Blue. "Hi," I tell Percy.

He takes a screw from the easel's lone leg. "Haven't seen you in detention lately."

"I'm too busy attempting to do good."

"Smart girl."

"I'm not too sure about that." I tug at a button on one of my pants pockets.

At the workbench, Percy takes out another screw. Unlike Kennedy, Percy appreciates silence. He gave me earplugs my freshman year and told me it was okay to turn off the noise. He also got the principal to okay my Red Rocket trees, and I gave him one of Macey's pies. We are friends. And, according to Kennedy Green, friends talk.

I tap my foot against my bag, the shark teeth jangling. "Were you really almost killed in the Gulf War?"

Percy slides the broken leg off the easel. "Where'd you hear that?"

"Kennedy Green, the girl who died last month. She said you told her you were in a convoy that was bombed in Iraq."

Percy picks up another broken easel. "Yep. She's got—I mean, she had—a way with people."

True. Dead and alive. At first I thought Kennedy was a moron, but she's far from dumb. I shake my head. "It's crazy, Percy. After only twenty minutes in detention, she got me to admit my greatest fears. And now she's got me . . . she's got me wondering about things."

Percy nods gravely.

"So why are you here, Percy? And I don't mean at this school or in this room. Why did you survive that roadside bomb in Iraq when others didn't?"

Percy takes the second easel apart and then works on a third and fourth, tossing the broken pieces into a large garbage bin. Finally he sets the screwdriver on a potter's wheel with a broken foot pedal, reaches into his pocket, and takes out a penny.

"You're not going to offer me a penny for my thoughts, are you?" I ask.

Percy drops the penny onto my hand. It's an old one, dulled and smoothed with time. I turn it over and try to make out the date: 1955. There's something odd about it. I study both sides. Lincoln's head is exactly where it needs to be, but the Lincoln Memorial is missing from the other side. Instead, two feathers curve the back side—no, not feathers. "Sprigs of wheat?"

"Yep. Wheat penny. Government stopped making them in 1958, so not many around these days. Got that one from my grandma. She told me it was good luck and to carry it with me wherever I go."

"And you do?"

"Yep. Had it with me in the Gulf."

I stare incredulously from Percy to the penny. "So you're saying you're here, you survived that roadside bomb, because of a lucky penny?"

"I'm saying there's a lot about this world we don't know and never will. Could be luck. Could be fate. Could be the spirit of old Abe himself keeping me safe." Percy folds my fingers over the penny. "But I'll hang my hat on a guardian angel."

I'm here for you.

Today Mr. Phillips wears a tie splattered with amoeba intestines. Squiggles of red curl in and out of brown and black smudges. No green. No blue.

Blue-green, the world's most perfect color.

Nate walks in and tosses his backpack onto my lab table. His fingers brush against mine. "Everything okay?" he asks. Of course he notices I'm in a thoughtful mood. I've been thinking about Kennedy and guardian angels, which is ludicrous, because the presence of a guardian angel would indicate the existence of a being in need of guarding, which would not be me. I grind the inside of my cheek with my back molars.

The tardy bell rings, and Mr. Phillips's lips move, but I don't hear what he says. Pennies are circles of copper, nothing more than a metal designated by the letters *Cu* on the periodic table. A good-luck penny did not save Percy. A guardian angel did not save Percy. The choices Percy made that day in the Gulf saved Percy. He chose that seat on that side of the convoy truck. He chose to wear his helmet and what to hold in front of his chest.

I pop my neck, jerking my head from one side to the other, and take out my biology notebook and pencil stub. I choose to arrive on time for biology. I choose to have Nate in my life. I choose to complete Kennedy's bucket list. Believing in fate and destiny and guardian angels doesn't make sense. I'm responsible for my successes and failures. Power comes from within, and the only person who can hold me back is me.

When the bell rings, signaling class is over, I toss my pencil into my bag. A large, pale hand settles on the top page of my notebook before I can close it.

"Ms. Blue." Mr. Phillips drums his index finger on the paper. "It saddens me that you find your time in biology a total waste."

"Excuse me?"

"Your . . . um . . . notes." He points to my notebook, covered in drawings of dozens of pennies. In most of them Lincoln wears horns, a mustache, or an arrow through his head.

"I have other things on my mind," I say.

"That's obvious." The amoebas on Mr. Phillips's tie pulse and swirl. He taps his pointer on his thigh and raises both eyebrows.

"What do you want from me—blood?" I ask.

Mr. Phillips sighs. "A bit more focus, work ethic, and respect would be nice."

"Fine." I rip the page from the notebook and tear it in half, again and again. "It's gone. All of it gone. Not a damned penny in sight!" I throw the pieces at the wastebasket, but most float about the room, landing on desks, the floor, and Mr. Phillips's shoe. "How's that?"

Mr. Phillips doesn't move at first. He sets his pointer on his desk and pulls a pink pad from his back pocket. "Detention. How's that?"

Ms. Lungren places a tattered box of crayons on my desk and one on Macey's. "Today you're going to get in touch with your artistic sides."

I should be ecstatic. Instead, I curse myself as I raise my hand.

"Yes, Rebecca?"

"I have track practice this afternoon. Is it possible to make other arrangements?"

"The track team will have to wait."

Life's a bitter bitch. For the first time in detention, I get to do something artistic, and all I can think about is my promise to my cousin. It's day two of track practice, and already I'm failing to "just show up."

But the thing that pisses me off the most is that I care.

"Sometimes words fail us," Lungren says. "They don't

adequately allow us to express our feelings, but that doesn't mean we should keep our feelings bottled inside, because when that happens, oftentimes you explode." She sets a large piece of white drawing paper on each of our desks. "I want you to draw a picture of the various feelings you experienced today, especially the strong feelings. Your artistic rendering can be of people or places or even words. Or you may choose a more abstract expression. The goal is to express your feelings in a safe and healthy way. Please get started."

Macey twirls a crayon, peachy orange. I dig through my box, my frown sharpening to a glare at the green crayon.

I push away the box and stand. "I need to use the bathroom."

Lungren nods. "Five minutes."

In the bathroom I steady my hands on the cold porcelain of the sink and inspect the girl in the mirror. Same blue streaks. Same sharky strap on my messenger bag. Same me. My forehead rests on the hard, smooth glass. But I don't feel like me. I bang my forehead against the mirror, the thud echoing through the bathroom.

The door swings open. Macey glides in and hoists herself up onto the other sink. "What's wrong?"

Peeling my face off the mirror, I turn on the water and cup my hands under the spray. "I kissed Nate, joined the track team, and made friends with a mom who uses cloth diapers."

"Is that supposed to make sense?"

"On some twisted level." And that's just it. Somehow my life got twisted into something I don't recognize. I splash water on my face, one handful after another, as if trying to wash away this person I've become. Macey turns off the water, and I rest my wrists on the sink.

"Seriously, how are you *feeling*?" Macey asks.

What is it about death that makes people want to talk about *feelings*? After my mom died, Aunt Evelyn was obsessed with my feelings, and ever since Kennedy died, I've been asking Macey about her feelings and talking to a total stranger about her feelings concerning laundry. The truth is, life was much easier when I chose to keep my feelings to myself and my nose out of other people's lives.

I fling my hands, water flying and my wrists clanking on the counter. "I'm angry."

"I get that, but there's usually something under the anger."

"More anger. I'm really, *really* angry."

"No, it's like . . ." Macey tugs at a long, ghosty lock of hair hanging along the side of her face. "It's like pie. Anger is the crust, and below the crust is the filling, which is really the heart of the pie. The crust masks something deeper, stuff like sadness or fear."

I cradle my face in my hands. "I'm not sure I can handle pie therapy right now."

"Try it."

I lift my head and glare at her. "Fine. I'm mad at Mr. Phillips because he gave me another detention."

"And?"

"I'm pissed off because I'm missing track practice."

"But what's below all that anger?"

I roll my neck along my shoulders. "Okay. I'm tired of battling Mr. Phillips. I feel guilty about letting down Pen and the track team. I'm worried Aunt Evelyn will take away my scooter." And after talking to Percy this morning, I'm confused about pennies and higher beings and guardian angels.

Some people are afraid of death and what lies beyond.

Shut up, Kennedy! And then there's Kennedy. I can't get her out of my head, and because of my vow to complete her bucket list, I can't get her out of my life. A dead girl's taking over, and I'm losing control. It's driving me insane.

Macey cranks the paper-towel handle, turning and turning. "Uh, that's a lot of feelings."

"You think?" My head is spinning, and I wrap my fingers around the edge of the sink to keep from sinking to the floor. "Do you believe in a higher being, Mace, that something has power over us and the choices we make?"

Macey continues to crank the handle, but the circular motion grows slower and jerkier. "I believe there's a lot of bad in the world, bad things most of us can't manage on our own. So, yeah, I believe in something good and big enough to battle the bad."

"And stuff like that makes me even more confused. I feel like my world's been rocked." By a bucket list that's not my own. A growl gurgles up my throat. "So what do I do, Macey? What do I do with all these stupid feelings?"

She tears off the paper towel and hands me the three-foot length. "You can help me bake pies."

A laugh puffs over my lips as I take the giant paper towel and wipe my hands. "Make pies?"

"Because sometimes you need something warm and sweet and comforting. Sometimes you just need pie."

I wad up the paper towel and lob it into the trash. Not much in my world is making sense, but somehow pie does. "How did you come up with this pie and anger stuff?"

"Years of therapy."

I picture the faint white lines on the undersides of her arms. "And it helped you? All those years of therapy?"

Macey slips her hands into her hoodie pockets. "I think I'm making more progress with pies." She leans against the door and pushes it open. "They're . . . uh . . . changing my life."

Change. My world is changing, too. Nate. The track team. Flash mobs.

Together Macey and I walk back to the detention room. I turn into the doorway, but she keeps walking.

"Hey," I call out. "We have another hour and forty-five minutes of detention. Where are you going?"

"The bake-off is in two weeks, and this afternoon all the competitors get to tour the event kitchens and confirm final supply and equipment lists."

"But you can't bail out of detention. Not again. Lungren will go postal."

Macey's ghost of a smile is back. "I don't have detention today."

After detention, I dash to the track as the team is starting their cooldown. I find Coach Evil. "I'm sorry I missed practice. I had detention. What do you want me to do?"

The coach tilts her chin toward my knee, still bandaged but no longer throbbing in pain. "Give it a rest today. Show up tomorrow, and we'll put you through a full workout."

"That's it?"

She looks mildly surprised, like you might upon finding a twenty-dollar bill in the pocket of a pair of jeans you dig out when the weather cools. "Thanks for checking in, Rebecca."

I don't head for the showers, where Pen will most likely be frowning and where Neanderthal Boy lurks under the bleachers. My pink sneakers looped over my shoulder, I head for the beach.

It's late afternoon, and I have plenty of time left to squeeze in another bucket-list item, but just like I need to rest my sore knee, I need a break from bucket lists, from acting out another girl's dreams and desires. I need to be me, a blue-haired, barefoot girl who likes sand between her toes.

Today the beach is full of people. College-age students play beach volleyball, and a dozen kids build sand castles. I find a quiet section where the sand is coarser, the waves stronger, and here I hunt for the sea's tears. I walk along the high-tide line among the pebbles, shells, and seaweed, prime real estate for sea glass. After a half mile, I spot a wedge of orange, and a tingle races up my spine. Orange sea glass is extremely rare, and I've yet to find a piece. I bend over and dig, unearthing a faded plastic milk cap. With a sigh, I stuff the trash into my pocket and keep searching. The sun starts to sink, but still I walk.

I meander along the shore past the grassy dunes until I reach the mudflats, and I realize I'm no longer searching for sea glass. I scan the flats and surrounding dunes and bushes for a pair of dimples that are sweeter and warmer than pie, but I don't see Nate. He's been checking the nesting habitat a few times every day, anxious to see if the migrating birds will adopt the improved grounds, but I must have missed him.

I'm about to leave when I see a flash of orange in the brush on the near side of the flats. Most likely another piece of trash. A bush with waxy, gray-green leaves shakes, and seconds later, a small gray bird with an unmistakable orange beak and black cap shoots from the leaves. I reach for my phone to take a picture, but the sea swallow darts over the dunes and disappears. But I saw that orange beak and can't wait to tell Nate.

Inside the Bolivar house, Nate's in the kitchen helping Nate the Younger with math. Somewhere Violin Girl plays slow, waltz-like music.

"I saw a sea swallow today at the mudflats," I say as I walk into the kitchen.

Nate looks up with an excited expression. "They're here?"

"Just one, but I'm sure it was one of the endangered birds. Looked just like the decoys we painted."

"Sounds like we need to celebrate," he says with a lift of both eyebrows. "Let me finish up with Mateo."

A hand settles on my leg, and I look down to see the tiniest Bolivar. "I lit a candle for you at Mass this week." His fingers slip into my hand. He's so serene, so holy.

"Uh . . . why?"

He tugs on my hand, and I bend so we're eye level. "Because I care about your soul."

"Oh . . . that's nice."

Gabby walks in. Today she wears a black beret with black leggings, a black T-shirt, and ballet slippers, nailing a sixties vibe. She thrusts a sketch pad at me. On the page is a hand-drawn dress. "What do you think?"

Nate cranes his head and looks over my shoulder. "I don't think it would look good on me."

Gabby swats him, and I laugh.

"It's for me," Gabby says with a stomp of her slippered foot. "It's my prom dress."

"You're going to a prom for ten-year-olds?" I ask.

"No, silly. It's for my prom when I'm in high school."

"And you're designing it now?"

"Of course. Here's what I had in mind for colors." She holds up a large ring with squares of fabric attached and selects a deep, rich red color, like the raspberries Macey and I saw in our trek to the farmers' market last weekend.

I squint at Gabby. "Perfect."

"I'm so glad you think so." She throws her arms around my waist and hugs. I'm not sure what to do with my hands. Patting her head seems weird. I stand like a scarecrow with Gabby on one side, Saint Boy on the other. At last Gabby pulls away. "So when do I get blue hair?"

"What did your mom say?"

Her lips press into a pout. "Like what she says matters."

"Yes, Gabby, it does." Aunt Evelyn cried the day I walked out of the bathroom with a streak of Electric Blue #1111 in my hair. My mom would have loved blue hair, and I liked to think my art-loving father would too. Gabby looks at the floor. "Well?"

"Mom said no. She said it's against the school dress code and will damage my hair." Her hands ball into fists. "I told her you have beautiful hair and she's a moron."

"No, you didn't. Please tell me you didn't say that to your mom."

"Of course I did. I'm mad as hell."

Another household disrupted by my wrecking ball of destruction. *You were right, Cousin Pen.*

Nate unlatches Gabby's tentacles and gives her shoulders a gentle shove. "Go channel some of your energy into Tia Mina's new dance dress." He points to Mateo. "You, math." And he points to me. "You and me, back patio."

Outside on the patio, I stand on the bottom step. Before me stretches a giant backyard with wagons and bikes and scooters scattered among lawn chairs and a fire pit. In one corner, there's a small plastic swimming pool, in the other a horseshoe pit. A place of chaotic happiness. Even the saint statue standing in a bed of flowers is smiling. He wears a long robe with a bird on his shoulder and deer at his feet.

I stand on the patio, frowning. "I'm teaching your little sister to swear and yell at your mother. This is not good, Nate, not good at all."

"Families fight, and they make up."

"But Gabby's obsessed with this blue-hair thing."

"No worries, Reb. I'll talk to Mom when she cools off." Because, like Kennedy, Nate has a way with people.

I rub a knuckle on the railing. "I'm a screwed-up person."

Nate puts his arms around my shoulders, pulling my back into his chest. He feels solid, warm, and good. "We all are."

"But some of us are more screwed up than others. I'm letting you know I'm definitely on the far right-hand side of the bell curve on this one."

He runs his fingers along the strap looped across my chest. "It makes you more interesting."

I tilt my head, looking up at him with doubt. "Interesting is good?"

He brushes his lips against the top of my head. "Interesting is amazing."

I sink back against the wall of his chest, matching my breathing with his and smiling as our hearts beat in sync. He rests his chin on the top of my head. I wish I could freeze this moment. Nothing else exists. No detention. No skinned knees and evil track coaches. No gropers under the bleachers. No doubts about who controls my life. No voice of a dead girl in my head. Just Nate and me and the beating of our hearts.

The door flies open, and Gabby runs onto the patio. "Mom called. She's going to be late and needs you to pick up Tia Mina at the dance studio."

"Duty calls," Nate says, but he doesn't move.

"And you are most dutiful." I drag myself from his arms and climb the steps so we're face-to-face. I slide my fingers through his hair and pull him toward me, pressing myself against him. "I think you're pretty amazing, too." I brush my lips across his, and everything bad and ugly and confusing ceases to exist.

When I pull away, he pulls me back. A dimple carves either side of his mouth. "Go to prom with me, Rebel."

"Ha-ha," I say. "I needed a laugh today, especially after getting detention and missing track practice." The muscle along the back of his jaw twitches, and if I weren't so close, I wouldn't have noticed it. "You are joking, aren't you? Please tell me you're joking." Sweat pops up along the back of my neck.

He loops his arm around my shoulders. "Of course."

15. Ride a Vespa through the Roman Forum

CHAPTER
SIXTEEN

"NO, REBEL, NO, NO, NO!" COACH EVIL STANDS ON the track, waving her hands. "You can't slow down for the baton pass. You're throwing off the other runner."

"Heaven forbid I do that," I say under my breath as I jog back to the start line. You'd think after sixty-five tries, I'd be able to hand off a baton to a teammate. I assume the ready position at my start line.

Pen, who's been practicing long, graceful jumps for the past hour in the sandpit to my right, jogs over to the line. "You're close, Reb," she says. "It's all about timing and rhythm and muscle memory. Pay attention to your rhythm. Count your steps if you need to."

I wipe the sweat from my temples and nod. The coach blows the whistle, and I take off. I pump my arms, keeping the baton straight and steady. As I approach the next runner, she takes off. I watch her legs, matching my stride to hers. One, two, three, four. No slowing, no hesitation. My muscles know what to do because, for the past two days, Coach Evil has been pounding it into my head. Five, six, seven, eight. I hold my hand in an inverted V and swing the baton forward. I keep my feet in motion, in sync with my teammate. Up goes the baton. Up goes my face.

Someone stands near the finish line waving me on, her blond, perky ponytail bouncing furiously.

Smack! The baton bounces off my teammate's nose. She tumbles to the ground, and I fall over her. I scramble to my hands and knees and look at the finish line, but no one's there. My confusion is quickly giving way to something hotter and sharper.

With this fall, there's blood. My teammate is fine, but a long scrape stretches down my forearm. "Go see the trainer," the coach says. What she means is, *Go far, far away.*

I drag the towel across my face, mopping sweat and the sheen of humiliation. Liia, the trainer, checks out the scrape on my arm. "How bad did I look?" I ask.

"Maybe you'll do better at middle distance," Liia says. "I think we have room for one more runner in the 3,200-meter."

"Isn't that like a mile or something?"

"Closer to two."

I stretch out on my back and watch the sky. Clouds have been forming, and a brisk wind has picked up, but we haven't had a spring storm lately, not the kind that rips the sky and weeps for an hour and then disappears. My eyelids droop closed. If I were the crying type, I'd have swollen eyes by now. As the coaching staff of the award-winning Del Rey School women's track-and-field team has learned over the course of two weeks, I'm not a hurdler, sprinter, or jumper. I can't throw things without damaging myself and others, and I've turned the 4 x 100 relay into a contact sport. When it comes to track-and-field, I'm an epic fail.

Liia finishes with my arm and sits on an overturned five-gallon bucket. "Why are you here, Rebel?"

I rest my bandaged arm on my stomach. Joining the track team was a way to get thirty straight days of random acts of kindness. Then it became a matter of being true to my word. I'd promised to just show up, and I will, but now, things are blurrier. Pen is counting on me. The bungalow is more peaceful, and I can't stop hearing Kennedy's voice. That, more than anything, is eating at me. But it's not just her voice. I'm smelling her and seeing her. I massage my head. The whole thing is making my brain ache. "Let's just call it a random act of kindness."

When I open my eyes, I turn onto my side and notice Liia's leg. It's a uniform "flesh" color and smooth as glass. Two strips of metal curve around the part of her leg just below the knee. It doesn't look human. I must make some kind of sound because Liia taps her calf against the bucket, and a hollow *thud* echoes.

"A random act of drunkenness," she says as she pushes down her sock, reveals a length of plastic, and unscrews her leg.

A breath catches in my throat. "What happened?"

"I was jogging one evening the summer before my sophomore year, and a drunk driver ran a red light and clipped me."

"That's horrible."

"Yeah, I thought so at first, but here's the crazy part. The accident was the beginning of my track career. I run in a league for athletes with disabilities and got a full scholarship to my number one college. I've come to believe that this"—she points to the plastic and metal—"is part of my journey. It's not what I planned, and it certainly hasn't been without pain, but I believe there's a higher being or unseen force that places us where we need to be when we need to be there."

I throw my hands over my ears. *You are dead, Kennedy, and I'm making a choice. I'm banishing you from my head. This is it. No more.*

You don't look well. Do you need something?

Something soft and warm presses into my shoulder.

Liia. It must be Liia, the trainer. I look at my shoulder and see the heavy polyester fabric of my uniform tank shift, but Liia's hands are busy strapping back on her leg. I stand, my legs unsteady, as if I'd run two miles. "I . . . I . . . need to go."

I don't bother to change. On my two-mile run from school to the bungalow, my feet pound the pavement, the *thwack* loud and real and completely of my own making. When I get home, I toss my backpack at one of the brass hooks in the kitchen.

"Rebecca, pick that up!"

I race up the ladder to my studio and sit in the window seat, watching the fleeting sun set the wall of glass picture frames on fire.

I believe there's a higher being or unseen force that places us where we need to be when we need to be there.

Shut up, Kennedy! Liia. *I mean shut up,* Liia!

Who said the same thing as Kennedy.

Who couldn't have touched my shoulder.

Fragmented bits of light tumble through the attic. I hop up from the window and begin to pace through the fractured light. Kennedy knew Liia because Kennedy was no track-team superstar. She was a support person, and she probably helped Liia when the trainer needed an extra set of hands. That makes sense. I'll bet every jar of sea glass I have that Liia and Kennedy had more than one conversation about fate and destiny and life after death.

None of which I believe in.

I'll hang my hat on a guardian angel.

"Please, Percy, not you, too."

I slide my palm along my shoulder. But I felt heat. I saw the dip in the heavy polyester fabric.

I'm here for you.

"Nope, not going there," I say aloud. "It was the wind."

"Who are you talking to?"

My hands drop to my sides as Penelope pokes her head through the door in the floor.

"Did you hit your head with the discus again?" Penelope asks.

"Ha-ha."

Pen rests her arms on the door opening. "I'm not joking, Rebel. Liia said you left practice early. She was worried she said something to upset you. She wanted to make sure everything's okay."

"I'm fine."

"She thought maybe she freaked you out with her leg."

"I'm fine."

"Because Liia is a nice person, and I don't want you treating her like a freak and hurting her feelings."

"Dammit, Pen. I'm fine with Liia. I'm fine with her leg. I'm even fine with the discus. Got that? I'm fine."

Pen's face folds in a frown, and she disappears down the ladder.

No lies.

Shut the fuck up, Kennedy!

The best way to get Kennedy out of my head is to get her bucket list out of my life.

I point to the repaired easels and boxes sitting in Percy's maintenance closet. "Do you think you can get all of it into the back of your dad's truck?" I ask Nate.

Nate squints at the art supplies and nods.

"Even the potter's wheel? It's awkward and heavy."

Nate puts one arm around my shoulders, pulls me to his side, and brushes his lips against the side of my head. "Even the potter's wheel."

I push him away. "Stop it."

"Stop what?"

"Hanging all over me."

"Past experience tells me you like it." He nuzzles my hair with his chin.

"Stop being a pain in the ass."

"You shouldn't swear," he murmurs against my ear.

I elbow him in the chest in a nonplayful way. "I'm serious, Nate. I don't want you to do that."

"Really?"

"No, not here."

We're standing in the doorway of the maintenance closet at the end of Unit One. It's Friday after school, and most of the student body has gone home. However, a few upperclassmen stand at the bulletin board posting prom posters.

"All right, Reb." Nate steps back and throws his palms into the air. "Tell me what you want, then. Tell me exactly what you want." He sounds snappish. Today he wears his baseball-practice clothes. Sweat and dirt ring his collar.

"I'm sorry," I say. He had a tough practice, and he's tired. "I'm in a bad mood and taking it out on you. I can get Percy to help."

Nate runs a hand through his hair. The sides stick out like straw from a scarecrow's hat. "No, I want to help." He surveys the art supplies and nods. "So tell me again, what are you doing with all this stuff?"

I explain that Miss Chang, my art teacher, cleaned out the art supply room, and Percy rescued and fixed some of the supplies. The easels won't fit in the attic crawl space, so I can't use them, but someone could, some needy elementary school or scout group. Kennedy would know where to find little people in desperate need of art supplies. "I stopped by the guidance center, and Lungren gave me the name of an after-school program for at-risk kids," I tell Nate.

"Sounds like the seeds of a 501(c)(3) charity."

"Yeah, something like that." I shift through the old easels. "Are you *sure* you can fit all of this in the truck? It's pretty bulky."

Nate squints. He does that when he's deep in thought, while staring at a twenty-five-foot sailboat that will someday be his, while painting bird decoys, while looking at me. "Yeah, we're good." So true. Nate is good, a good student, a good son, a good kisser.

"And you can help me deliver them on Saturday?"

"No worries. Got everything under control."

That makes one of us. "Then let's go to the beach." I need to feel warm sand slipping between my toes.

"I don't get it," I say.

Nate makes an *mmm* sound.

"We cleared the weeds. We set up the decoys. We built the chick condos and fencing. You alone spent more than a hundred hours on the nesting site. The rest of the birds should be here by now."

"Mmm."

I thwack him on the chest. "The nesting grounds, Nate. Look at the nesting grounds. Except for that one bird on the fence post, they're empty." He hauls himself out of my lap, where he's been resting with his eyes closed and toying with the tips of my hair. I point to the mudflats we've been working on for the past month. "It's mid-May, and the birds should be here. It's weird."

He squints at the mudflats. "You're right. It's weird." He settles back into my lap.

"And you're not worried?" I ask.

"Reb, the birds will get here when they get here."

"But—"

"I have faith."

I picture the gold chain hanging at his neck, the one that holds the tiny gold cross. Nate has faith. He's the one who suggested there was something on Kennedy's list that I, and only I, needed to complete, and he believes I will complete the list because I'm true blue.

My fingers glide up to the thick, lush folds of his hair. It's so easy to be with Nate. That's what's making my life bearable. With Nate there's no track-team humiliation, no fights with school admin about trees, no possessed bucket list taking over my life.

He loops a curl of my hair around his finger. "Go to prom with me."

"The first time was funny. The second time is annoying."

He rolls out of my lap and sits, facing not the ocean, but me. "I'm serious, Rebel. You talk about living your truth, and you pointed out how most people are less than honest, including me. The truth is, Reb, there's not another girl in the world that I want to dance with right now." Nate's dark eyes are clear, intense.

I pick at a seam of my cargo pants.

"Now your turn." Nate takes my hand, lacing his fingers with mine. "Tell me the truth. Is there anyone you'd rather tango with?"

"All right, I'll say it. There is no one I'd rather dance with than you." I stare at our intertwined hands, a good fit. "But I won't go to prom."

Nate's hand tenses. "Why not?"

"I'm not a prom kind of girl."

"But I'm a prom kind of guy." One side of his mouth crooks in a half smile, and I catch my breath. He plucks a spray of purple wildflowers from a sandy part of the outcrop and runs the bell-shaped flowers along my leg. "And don't say you didn't enjoy our tango."

Yes, we've tangoed, and I enjoyed being in Nate's arms, but this whole prom thing isn't about dancing. "Think this through, Nate. Can you picture me at a prom? If there were a gathering of Children of the Anti-Prom, I'd be the poster child. I hate dresses and can't walk in high heels. I can't dance. I'm not good at small talk and ooing and aahing over sparkly new shoes. I would be the world's worst prom date. You wouldn't have fun with someone like me."

"It's just a dance." The petals slide along my arm.

"Drop it, Nate, please. I'm not up to this discussion today."

"But I am, and I want you to tell me why you're so dead set against going to prom."

"It's just not my world."

"It's mine."

"So I should forget all about who I am and what I stand for to make you happy?"

"For one night, Reb, why not?"

"Shouldn't the question be *why?* Why is it so important for me to go to prom with you? Do you need me to prove something to you or all those other people you care so much about? *Hey, world, look at us! We're a couple.*"

"What's wrong with that?"

"We're not a couple."

The flowers still at my shoulder. "Really?"

"Don't look at me like that."

Nate drops the spray of flowers. "Exactly what are we, Reb?"

"We're friends. We know how to tango and kayak together. And we have warm, fuzzy feelings for each other." I burrow my toes into the sand. "But whatever we are, we're temporary."

"Says who?" Nate's tone is sharp.

"Why are you in such a pissy mood?"

"You're the one raising your voice."

"I'm not yelling!" I wrap my hand around the shark teeth on my bag. "Listen, I'm not doing this right because I don't under-stand how things like this work. Sometimes—hell, most of the time—I don't get the rules. The rules about relationships and math and when it's okay to lie. You get that, don't you? That's the real problem here. I'm not good at interacting with people. I didn't get the memo. I slept through all the class lectures." I try to cajole a smile from him.

"I'd say we're doing pretty good." His lips remain stick straight.

"But it can't last."

"Because . . . ?"

I drop my head into my hands. Because the person Nate is falling for isn't me. For the past month I've been acting out Kennedy's dreams and desires. I've been hanging out with her friends, running on her team, and doing her good deeds. I've been living her life.

In my head I know I'm not a runner, I'm not a do-gooder, and I'm definitely not the prom type. But the crazy thing is, I'm enjoying my early-morning runs, I'm finding joy in doing for others, and I love to dance in Nate's arms. Which is the heart of the issue. I have no idea who the hell I am anymore. I've not only lost me, I've lost control.

Two months ago I would have sworn on my mother's grave that I'm in charge of my own fate, my own destiny, but now Kennedy and Percy and Liia and even Macey have me thinking about forces out of my control. It's like I'm racing down a steep mountain on Nova and her brakes just crapped out.

"Because . . . ?" Nate prompts again.

I shake my head, a lock of blue falling over my left eye. How do you explain crashing and burning to a guy who has everything under control? There's no way I should get into any kind of relationship right now. "We're too different."

"Different can be good. We complement each other."

"But at a fundamental level, we're at odds. You said it yourself. I'm true blue." I need to put on the brakes. Smacking the sand from my feet, I stand.

He unwinds his legs. "Are you calling me a liar?"

I sling my bag over my head, the shark teeth scratching my neck. "You said it, not me."

"But that's what you mean, right?"

"I need to go." I thrust my feet into my flip-flops. Nate pounces, planting himself right in front of me, and I have no place to go but over the cliff. "Fine. You want it straight? I'll give it to you. You're not living your own life, Nate. You can't tell people no."

"What the hell does that mean?"

"You can't tell Mr. Phillips you don't want to help me with my lab assignment."

"I was being respectful."

"You can't tell your baseball coach you don't want to do another round of batting practice."

"Forgive me for being committed."

I rush on, my gunfire words giving him no time to speak, because what I'm saying is unabashedly true, and we both know it. "You don't even want to go to college and get an MBA. You want to sail away on a boat to a place where for a moment in time you don't have work or expectations or responsibilities. And you're scared shitless to tell your father the truth." I raise my hands to my mouth, trying to pull back the words, not because they aren't true, but because Nate looks like he's been slammed with a wrecking ball.

The skin across his jaw tightens and whitens. The side of his mouth twitches, as if he's biting back words. At last he clears his throat and steps aside. "I'll drive you home."

"Wait, Nate, that didn't come out right."

I reach for his arm, but with his athletic grace, he sidesteps my touch. He takes off toward the parking lot.

"No worries," he says, and for the first time, I don't believe him.

16. Ride an inflatable turkey in the Macy's Thanksgiving Day Parade

CHAPTER
SEVENTEEN

"HERE'S THE BOX." I DROP A FOOT-SQUARE, STAIN-less steel box onto the kitchen table.

"Do you think it will be big enough?" Aunt Evelyn asks.

Uncle Bob takes the cap off the can of epoxy and nods. "I'm sure it will be fine."

Yep, everything is fine, if I ignore the fact that Nate agreed we have a nonrelationship. He no longer meets me at my locker for lunch, nor does he wait for me after track practice. I sit at the mudflats waiting for the swallows alone. No, not alone. Kennedy's bucket list is never far away. It's pushing at my back and shouting in my head. Sometimes I want to push back, to shout, *Get the hell out of my world!*

"What now, Reb?" Uncle Bob asks.

Aunt Evelyn wiggles her fingers, her silver bead bracelet tinkling. "This is so exciting."

Penelope digs through a large plastic tub marked *School Days*, rummaging around for items to complete another task on Kennedy Green's bucket list.

Make a time capsule with my family.

A time capsule holds bits and pieces of the present that will be hermetically sealed and opened sometime in the future. This is one of the items near the end of Kennedy's list, one dredged from the deepest, darkest part of her heart, because when she dug deep, Kennedy Green found family.

I slash a jagged check on the next item on the time capsule supply checklist. "Who has the label?"

"That's me!" Aunt Evelyn takes out a hand-lettered label that reads *Do Not Open Until 2033*. A swirly border surrounds the perfectly crafted letters. "Where do you want it? On the top or front?"

"Front," Pen says.

Aunt Evelyn waits for my confirmation. I nod, and she holds the label below the front clasp and frowns. "Does this look straight?"

Next to the word *Label*, I make another jagged check mark.

"Looks good," Uncle Bob says.

Aunt Evelyn wrinkles her nose. "It looks crooked to me. Maybe it's the lettering. Pen?"

"Perfect."

"Rebecca?"

"Just put on the stupid label." I take a deep breath. "Please. Here are some bags. If you have anything where the ink may bleed or that could get fragile with age and fall apart, put it in a plastic bag."

"Good idea, Rebecca," Aunt Evelyn says. "Isn't that a good idea, Bob?"

"Good idea." Uncle Bob inserts the epoxy glue into a trigger gun. "Now let's put everything into the box."

I open the lid.

"No!" Aunt Evelyn waves her hands in alarm. "One at a time, so we can hear what's important to each of us." Aunt Evelyn's cheeks are flushed, her tone cheerful. "You go first, Bob."

Uncle Bob sets aside the epoxy gun and drops in the front page of a newspaper, one of his pay stubs, a grocery store receipt, and a postage stamp. "Everyday stuff, but it gives a good snapshot of world affairs and the economy."

"Excellent!" Aunt Evelyn claps her hands. "Now my turn." She hauls out a handful of photographs. Pen and me in Halloween costumes. Pen playing soccer. Me building a sand castle. She adds letters, one to Uncle Bob, one to Penelope, one to me, and one labeled *Grandkids*. With a happy little hum, she slips in last year's Christmas letter, a hand-knitted pot holder, a rooster salt and pepper shaker set, and a decorating magazine.

When it's Pen's turn, she holds up a friendship bracelet.

"Because friendships, in any decade, are important."

I throw the bracelet into the steel box. "Next."

"Rebecca, don't be rude," Aunt Evelyn says. "This is supposed to be a fun family project."

But you're not my family, are you? The words lodge in my chest, heavy bricks pressing against my heart.

Uncle Bob uncaps the epoxy. "Okay, Pen, let's get this show on the road. What's next?"

Penelope adds photos and a team roster from track, tickets from a concert, last semester's report card, a dried corsage from the Mistletoe Ball, and a picture and sales tag for the dress she bought for prom.

Aunt Evelyn settles her hand on my arm. "Are you okay, Rebecca? You look a little flushed. Do you want me to turn on the fan?"

"No."

Pen adds more items, but I'm too busy thinking about the item I won't be adding, a picture of my prom dress. Because I'm not going to prom.

I focus on Pen, who's trying to stuff a small doll into the time capsule. "Why are you putting that in?"

"Polly Pockets are an iconic item from my childhood. I used to play with them for hours."

"There's no room, Pen."

"I'm sure we can fit it in if I do a little rearranging," Uncle Bob says.

"Or maybe we should get a bigger box," Aunt Evelyn suggests. "This one is not a good fit. Rebecca hasn't put her stuff in yet. By the way, Rebecca, are you sure you only want to put in sea glass and black jelly beans? Don't you have something more meaningful?"

"Reb's stuff is fine, and so is the box," Uncle Bob says.

"Look." Aunt Evelyn jabs a hand at the pile of things in front of Penelope. "Pen has more stuff to add. This box isn't going to work."

"This is the box Rebecca chose, and this is *her* project. Pen will need to include fewer items. Pen, hon, why don't you take out a few that may be not as important?"

"They're all important to her, or she would not have brought them." Aunt Evelyn grabs the doll from Penelope and shoves it headfirst into the overflowing box.

"It won't fit there." Uncle Bob sounds exasperated.

"We can make it fit." Aunt Evelyn jams harder. The neck snaps, and the head rolls across the table.

A cry escapes from Pen's throat.

Aunt Evelyn drops the doll body.

Uncle Bob swears under his breath.

I pick up the doll parts and tuck them in separate corners. "Problem solved." I toss in my sea glass and jelly beans and slam the lid, but some of the sea glass tumbles out.

Pen reaches for her postcards. "I want to include these."

"Won't fit."

"Sure they will. They're flat. I can slide them in the space in the back."

"Nope." I hold out my hand to Uncle Bob. "Glue, please."

"What the hell is your problem?" Pen demands.

Aunt Evelyn raises both hands, her bracelet slipping and pinching the fleshy part of her forearm. "Girls, please—"

"No," Pen says. "There's room for my postcards."

"This argument is stupid," I say. "This whole thing is stupid."

"Then maybe we shouldn't do it." Pen pushes her chair back and stands. "Maybe we should forget the whole stupid thing."

We can't, because Kennedy Green won't let me. I summon my last bit of patience from an unknown depth. "You're right. We can fit the postcards in the back. Let's get this finished."

"So you can tick off another item from Kennedy's bucket list? Don't forget, Reb, I read the list. I know exactly what you're doing. The only reason you're making a time capsule with *my* family is because a dead girl wanted to make a time capsule with *her* family." She turns to her parents. "She doesn't even want to be here. You realize she's using us."

Aunt Evelyn folds her hands on the rooster place mat in front of her. "Rebecca, what is Pen talking about?"

I fold the checklist and smooth out the crease. "Honestly?"

Pen snorts. "With you, there's no other way." She uses her snippy, know-it-all voice, the same voice her bratty little ten-year-old self used to make it clear I didn't belong in her bedroom, classroom, or on her soccer team. I didn't know how to deal with it then, and I still don't, other than with the truth.

"Yes, Pen, this was on Kennedy's bucket list, and you're right, I don't want to be here at this table, because I don't fit in with this family." My hands sink to my lap, and the time capsule checklist flutters to the ground. "I never have. I've never been smart enough or athletic enough. I don't wear the right clothes or eat food-pyramid-approved breakfasts. I don't belong."

"If you're trying to shock us, sorry, Reb, major fail," Pen says. "You've made it clear exactly how you feel about this family. We all get that. Well, here's a news flash. We don't want you here, either." Pen swings her arm across the table, and the steel box crashes to the floor, the contents scattering.

Uncle Bob stares at the epoxy glue gun. Aunt Evelyn gasps. I can't move. With a choky sob, Pen runs from the room.

Aunt Evelyn runs after Penelope, and Uncle Bob drops the glue gun.

The clock ticks. Outside, Tiberius barks. But the loudest sound is my heart pounding against the wall of my hollow chest as I look at the spilled contents of the time capsule.

Rebecca, pick that up!

If I still smoked, tonight would be a full-pack night. I'd puff on one cigarette after another, creating a never-ending chain of ashy worms. But I threw away all my cigarettes a week ago, and now the idea of smoke clogging my throat and swirling about my lungs makes me want to puke. So tonight I slip into my pink tennis shoes, tie back my hair, stretch, and run.

Tonight Pen almost blew a vein, much like the day in the parking lot at Kennedy Green's Celebration of Life. But after Macey's pie therapy, I see what's below her anger: fear. Pen's afraid her parents will divorce and her family will fall apart because of me.

As for me, I don't hate Cousin Pen and Aunt Evelyn and Uncle Bob. I'm not angry. I . . .

I run faster, pretending a teammate runs in front of me, holding out her hand, waiting for the baton, which I pass off with perfect execution. I leap across imaginary hurdles. I run harder, pushing with my chest, as if I'm crossing a finish line. But the words in my head beat me.

I'm not angry at Aunt Evelyn and Pen. I envy them.

My pink tennis shoes screech to a halt. I bend over the knifelike pain in my stomach. I envy what they have. A family. Because I lost mine. On a cloudy day in March six years ago when my mother's Jeep plunged off a cliff while she'd been shooting photos in the mountains of Bolivia. The stitch jolts my entire body. I wrap my arms around my chest to stop the shaking, but I can't stop. I don't want to make a time capsule with Pen's family; I want to make one with my family, the mother who died and the father I never knew.

When I wake the next morning, the bungalow is unusually silent. Aunt Evelyn doesn't order me to sit down at a rooster place mat and eat a vegetable omelet. Pen doesn't complain about my leaving wet towels on my side of the room. And Uncle Bob doesn't grunt me a good morning from behind his newspaper. We shuffle past one another as if shell-shocked. We are the walking wounded. But all is not quiet. Kennedy yammers.

We all need friends.

This time, I don't argue. As I grab my bag and rush out the door, I have one thought on my mind: I need Macey. For the past three years Macey and I have been detention comrades and friends-of-convenience. But she cared enough about me to learn to ride a tandem, and I care about pies. I look for her before school but can't find her. During lunch period, I hurry to the FACS room and bite back a cry of relief when I spot her crouched in front of a cupboard, pulling out large bags of flour and sugar.

I hoist myself onto the counter and watch as she takes butter and a carton of blueberries from the refrigerator.

She places the pie ingredients in a bag and glides to the garbage can.

"Stop!" I say. "You're not going to throw that away, are you?"

"Uh, yes."

"Why?"

The veins on her wrist strain as she lifts the bag to the garbage can. "I'm not doing the bake-off."

"What? Why?" I run to the garbage can, blocking her way.

"Was there a problem at the meeting yesterday? Did you get disqualified or something?"

"No. I just don't want to do it anymore."

Macey walks past me but doesn't meet my gaze.

"Liar."

"Excuse me?"

"You can't lie to me, Macey. You worked hard this past month. You care about those pies."

She raises her arm, and the bag hovers over the trash can. "But I'm done."

I grab her arm. "If you throw away those bags, you're throwing away someone's dreams and desires. Yours."

"Reb—"

"And I'm not going to let you do that."

A bright wash of red fires Macey's face. "Who the hell are you to order me around?"

"I'm your friend, Macey, your best friend. Maybe you can't admit it yet, but you're mine. I get that you have a . . . a . . ."

. . . guarded heart.

I glare at the ceiling and clear my throat. ". . . a guarded heart. You try to keep people away, but not me. I've been at your side since that first detention our freshman year." My fingers claw around the bag. "The reality is, right now my life's pretty screwed up. I need something good, and you and peaches and pies are good. I've been here for you, and frankly, it's time for you to be here for me."

Macey eyes me warily, but she doesn't move away. "You need pie?"

I hug the bag to my chest. "You have no idea how much I need pie."

For the longest time, Macey tugs at the cuffs of her hoodie while I clutch the grocery bag to my heart. At last she walks back to her kitchen, where she pulls something out of her backpack. "Then I need your help." She holds up a T-shirt. "I went to the bake-off meeting, and the event organizers handed out these. They want us to wear them on the day of the bake-off, and . . ."

I take the shirt from her, my fingers wrapping around the short sleeves. ". . . and your scars will show."

". . . and that's the only thing people will see."

"So wear a long-sleeve shirt underneath."

"They won't let me." Macy's chalky face turns gray. "They're taping the whole thing, and parts of it will be used during the televised national bake-off. They want us all to match."

I don't bother turning to Kennedy for answers, because we don't need the ghost of a dead girl for this. "Like I said, Macey, everyone has scars, and some of us are just better than others at covering them up. After school today we'll go buy makeup."

Macey's entire face contorts in a frown. "Are *you* suggesting I cover the scars? That I hide them? What happened to being true to you?"

"You're not lying to yourself. You're not pretending the scars don't exist. You're just being selective about who you show your true self to."

Macey continues to roll the hoodie fabric around her hands. "Don't you have a track meet today?"

"Yes, but it doesn't start until four. We'll have plenty of time for a makeup lesson at Bella's."

17. Go to the equator and line dance

CHAPTER
EIGHTEEN

IF I BELIEVED IN A HIGHER BEING OR SOME GREATER force that determined my fate, I'd be pelting him or her with sharp objects.

Nova won't go.

I sit on my scooter in the parking lot at Bella's Discount Beauty Supply and crank the ignition switch again. Nothing. Dead battery? Dead carburetor? Dead something. I check my phone. The track meet begins in fifteen minutes. After getting makeup to hide her scars, Macey left Bella's and went to the farmers' market, and I'm supposed to be on my way to school. A city bus pulls up to the intersection a few doors down. Jamming my scooter key into my pocket, I dash to the corner. As I reach for the door, the bus belches and lurches forward.

"Come baaaaack." I wave, but the driver chugs off in a plume of smoke. No time to swear. I take off my flip-flops and run.

I arrive at school sweaty and winded, a stitch cramping my right side. As I jog through the parking lot near the gym and sports fields, I notice all the cars. Today's track meet is the qualifier before regionals.

After I change into my orange and yellow sporto outfit, I jog to the field and spot Coach Evil standing near the scoring table. "Sorry I'm late. I'm sorry, really, really sorry. My scooter died."

"Later, Rebel." Her hand swishes the air near my nose. "I'm reworking some numbers."

"Where should I go?" I ask.

She shows me the palm of her hand, so I jog to where Pen's standing with a group of Cupcakes. "Where do you want me? What should I do?"

Captain Pen's bottom lip quivers, but she says nothing. One of the Cupcakes settles her hand on Pen's shoulder. Another angles her body, as if protecting Pen from me.

"What's going on?" I ask.

A Cupcake waves a hand at the judging table. "You got DQ'd."

"DQ'd?"

"Disqualified."

"You failed to show for your 3,200-meter race." Pen's voice

is like cracked ice. "There's no way we can get top seed going into regionals without those bracket points."

Swear words fail me. "I'm so sorry." Forget the Rebel nickname. Call me Sorry. "What can I do to make it up? Do you want me to run another event? I'll even try the discus."

"Leave, Rebel. We don't need you."

On the walk home from the track, I pass Bella's Discount Beauty Supply. When I'd been there earlier in the day helping Macey find makeup to cover her scars, I hadn't noticed the giant pink posters announcing 50-percent-off deals in the windows. I'm not a shopper, not the sort of girl who needs a little retail therapy when slammed with wrecking balls, but since I don't smoke anymore, I need more hair dye. Nate needed prom. The track team needed promptness. And I failed to deliver. I screwed up because I don't understand the rules in this world; I don't fit in. From the moment I landed in Tierra del Rey, I had troubles fitting in, at school, in Uncle Bob's family, on soccer teams. I told myself it was fine, because being me was "fine" and the wrong would come when I stopped being me. I figured if they didn't like me, then I didn't need them. I'd spent the past six years pushing people away. Now Nate had pushed me away, my mom's family pushed me away, and the track team pushed me away. The other end of push-back hurts.

I buy three boxes of dye at Bella's, Electric Blue #1111, a splash of color that screams I'm okay with different. I'm okay with being a trapezoid in a round hole. I am not Kennedy Green. I am Rebel Blue.

This is me. This is good. And why not spread the goodness? I almost laugh out loud. *Kennedy, Kennedy, Kennedy. You're still hanging on.* I failed to help the track team today, but I can do something nice for a fashion diva who desperately wants blue hair and who is going to get it when school's out next month because Nate promised to smooth the way with his parents. Nate the Great doesn't fail.

Still in my tennis shoes and track outfit, I jog from the strip mall to Nate's house. Nate's oldest sister, the one who plays the violin, answers the door. "Nate's gone." She starts to close the door.

I wedge my shoulder into the doorway. "I'm here to see Gabby. Is she around?"

Nate's sister raises her violin, as if warding off danger.

I show her the bag from Bella's. "I have some hair stuff she wanted. That's all."

She taps her violin against her thigh and finally steps out of the doorway. "Gab, someone's at the door for you."

I wait in the entryway, the toe of my tennis shoe tracing the mosaic of colored tile. "Gabby," I call out.

Something thuds at the back of the house. I follow the twisting maze of brightly colored rooms. Tia Mina's at the kitchen table talking on the phone. Saint Boy sits at a desk playing a computer game featuring a talking tomato. I find Gabby in a back bathroom. She sits on the toilet, her head wrapped in a towel.

"Go away," she says, tears sliding down her cheeks.

"What happened?" I lunge across the bathroom and squat before her, grasping her hands. "Are you okay?"

She yanks her hands from mine. "Go away."

On the counter sits a gallon of bleach, the kind Aunt Evelyn stores in the laundry room, the kind used to get diapers snowy white. "You used *this* on your hair?"

A sob tumbles from her mouth.

"Hey, it's okay. I've been doing this dye stuff for years. We can fix it." I reach for the towel on her head. "Let's—"

She twists from my grasp. The sudden motion loosens the towel, which falls to a puddle on the floor. Shock steals every word racing up my throat. Locks of frizzy orange hair hang down either side of her face. A chunk of hair is missing from the back of her skull. The top of her right ear is red and blistered. "Oh, Gabby, let me—"

"Piss off!" Her hands curl into tiny shaking knots of rage.

I need to get her to a calm place. I hang the towel on a hook and wink at her. "Don't swear. It's not attractive and will keep you out of heaven."

Her cheeks flare with fiery red. "Go to hell!"

The words punch me in the gut, and I stumble backward. Gabby stands, pushes me out of the bathroom, and slams the door. The lock turns.

Something stands in the corner at the far end of the hall, but it's not a statue of a saint. It's Saint Boy. "I don't think she wants you here," Nate's youngest brother says.

Unwanted = Me.

I run from Nate's house in a blur of pink shoes. Burly clouds rumble in the sky as a gray mist starts to fall, but I continue to run. My throat aches and lungs burn, as if I smoked a hundred cigarettes, but there's no sweet peace or nicotine high.

When I reach the mudflats, I stop and catch my breath. Automatically I look for sea swallows. The mist has thickened into a fine drizzle, and the sky wraps about me like a heavy, sodden cloak. I squint through the gray but see no birds.

Where the hell are the birds? They should be here. They belong here.

Right here. Right now.

No, Kennedy, I can't deal with you right now.

Settling my back against a fence post, I slide to the ground. Pasty mud sucks at my running shoes. I yank off the shoes and awful orange socks. The shoes weigh heavy in my hand, like a pair of discuses. The drizzle thickens, and a raindrop plops onto my head. Another smacks my big toe. Within seconds, water pours from the heavens. Even the polyester track outfit abandons the fight. The shiny fabric coats me like a second skin, and still I sit with the stupid shoes in my hand, shoes that failed to *just show up.*

Once again, I've proven I'm only good at being bad.

Maybe Pen's right. Maybe I'm incapable of doing good.

No, I'm not going to give her that. I spent the past month doing small and not-so-small acts of goodness. I'm saving sea turtles and endangered birds, feeding the homeless, cleaning up beaches, starting a charity to supply children with art supplies, learning sign language to interpret for the deaf, and planting Red Rocket crepe myrtle trees.

"You see that, Pen? I'm good!"

But not when it comes to dealing with people.

I jump to my feet, and mud squishes through my toes. My hands curl around the shoes, crushing them. I spin and spin, winding up and gaining speed. At last I fling Pen's shoes out of my life and stumble to a stop so I can watch the shoes sink into the ocean, but I don't even get that satisfaction. The shoes smash into a stand of bushes, which scream and shiver and explode.

I cup my hands around my eyes, keeping the rain out and watching as birds, not leaves, fly from the bushes. There are dozens, maybe even a hundred, all with orange beaks. My heart stutters and takes off at the speed of fluttering wings. The sea swallows have finally arrived. A single thought rushes through my head: I wish Nate were here.

He's not because you pushed him away.

Because he wanted to go to a stupid dance. I don't need stuff like proms. I don't need to prove myself to anyone.

But you need him.

Says who?

You. You needed him after that second detention, and you needed him to help with Gabby. Just like you need Macey and Percy and a family, you need Nate.

I jump to my feet and slip on a rock, scraping my heel. "Get out of my head!"

You want his arms wrapped around you, and you don't want "temporary."

"Get out of my head, Kennedy Green. You have no right to be there. You're dead!" Tears well behind my eyes, and through the gray drizzle in my head I hear another voice.

I'm not Kennedy Green, you moron.

Boneless, I sink back to the mud. It's not Kennedy's voice. The last flutter of wings tapers off, and bits of gray fly back into the shrubs. A leaden pressure settles on my chest.

The voice is mine.

"You are so not normal," I say with a choked laugh. Normal people don't have conversations with themselves and dead girls. I press my fingertips into my eye sockets, rubbing until I see white and black splotches.

No, I'm not normal. I'm my mother's daughter. I march to the beat of my own 275-piece marching band. I can pull off blue hair and bare feet.

I stare at my feet, slick with mud and tears from the sky because I don't like shoes that pinch, shoes that bind, shoes that slow me down. That's where all of this starts, with shoes.

I'm a barefoot girl in a world that wears shoes.

And a month ago, I was fine with that. Now, for the first time in my life, that thought crushes me.

I want to dance in Nate's arms, I want to play on a team, I want to sit and eat dinner with a family. I want to belong, but the cold, hard truth is, no one wants me.

"Damn you, Kennedy!" I lift my face to the sky. "And damn your stupid list!"

18. Take a shower under a waterfall

CHAPTER
NINETEEN

AT SOME POINT, THE RAIN STOPS. THE CLOUDS split open, and a lance of light cuts through the gray. The light is bright, deeper than yellow: gold, a heavenly gold. My sobs give way to a creaky laugh that tumbles from a raw, gut-deep place.

"You don't give up, do you, Kennedy? And you will continue to annoy the crap out of me, even from the grave."

I pull myself upright and watch the golden light spill across the sky like an upended paint bucket. "Are you waiting for me to admit it, that you and I were destined to meet? That I was supposed to complete your list because something needed to be done? Or that I subconsciously was drawn to your list because it was full of things I desperately wanted?"

Kennedy doesn't answer. Nor does the sky.

But I don't need their answers, because the answers have always been in front of my face, written in twenty neat lines on a dead girl's bucket list. Almost all of Kennedy Green's bucket-list items deal with connecting with people: family, friends, even strangers. And I don't need Macey's shrink to tell me that my world was sorely lacking in those areas. What I don't understand is how the list ended up in my life. Was something deep in my subconscious hard at work? Was I nudged by a higher being, force of nature, God, or a guardian angel? I have no idea.

There's so much in this world I don't understand, stuff that my little human mind will never understand. My face lifts toward the warmth of the sun. So much light. So much world. So much unknown. I'm a tiny speck wanting to be seen and heard.

But for now, I don't need answers. Right now I need pie.

Macey's mom takes one look at me and pulls me into the house. "How about a hot shower?" Her tone is light, conversational. She may as well have said *How about a cup of chai tea?*

I don't argue. Something tells me she's seen this type of thing before. Macey's mom ushers me down a hall, and when Macey sticks her head out of a bedroom, she says, "Macey, dear, why don't you get Rebel a warm pair of sweats and a hoodie?"

Hot water rushes over my skin, soothing waves of warmth. Macey's soap smells of strawberries, and I welcome the sweet, clean scent. After I dry off and change, I find Macey in the kitchen, pulling a pie from the refrigerator.

I sit, and she hands me a fork. We don't bother with plates. The tines of my fork break the flaky crust. Inside is a riot of purple and red. "Is it wrong to be mad at a dead girl?" I ask around a mouthful of triple-berry pie.

"Feelings aren't right or wrong; they just are," Macey says as she licks her fork.

"More pie therapy?"

"Nope. That came from an actual therapist."

My fork plows through a quarter of the pie before I speak again. "So basically the world hates me, and it's all Kennedy's fault. Technically, it's the list's fault, but since she wrote the list, she shares the blame." I explain my revelation that by chance or subconscious choice, I took on Kennedy's bucket list because I needed people in my life. "It's just a stupid list, right? Carbon on tree pulp. A series of letters and punctuation. But it slammed me. It made me realize how empty my life has been since my mom died. So now I realize I want a family, I want a boyfriend—hell, I even want to be a member of a team. But in the end, no one wants me, Macey. Do you know what it's like to screw up so bad that no one wants to be around you?"

Macey runs the tines of her fork along a berry on the bottom of the pie plate. "It . . . uh . . . hurts."

I grab another forkful of pie. "Exactly, and it hurts to realize over the past few days that I hurt others. I hurt Nate, my family, the track team, and even little Gabby. Everything's a mess. I've failed at everything."

Macey shakes her head. "Not the bucket list."

"Macey, haven't you heard me? The bucket list is the root of all evil. It set me on this epic journey of failure."

"But you haven't failed the list. You've completed every item on the list you've tried, and as far as I know, you haven't yet given up."

I picture all the things I've done over the past month, from planting trees to learning sign language, and every day I completed a random act of kindness. She's right. So I'm saved from complete failure by Kennedy Green. I'm too exhausted to laugh. "But my life is filled with so much broken."

Crumbs line the pie plate when Macey finally speaks. "You can't fix everything right away. Some things take time."

"I know. Peaches." I want to rest my head on my arms and never leave this table. "But there are some things that need to be fixed right now." I stand. "Nova's being attitudinal. Do you have any wheels?"

Macey borrows her mother's car and drives me to Nate's house. Nate the Younger opens the door. "Nate's not here."

"I'm not here to see Nate. This is for your mom or dad or whoever has to deal with Gabby's hair." I hand him a piece of paper with the name and phone number of the manager at

Bella's Discount Beauty Supply. She taught me how to dye my hair, and at one time she worked at the local beauty academy. "I told her about Gabby's hair, and she said she can help."

He takes the paper and closes the door.

Macey drops me off at the bungalow, and for a moment I seriously consider hiding out in the attic, but that would just delay the inevitable. Sooner or later I'll have to face the nuclear fallout. I walk in and find Uncle Bob sitting at the kitchen table. I toss my bag at one of the brass hooks, but it falls to the floor with a sickening thud.

Uncle Bob flicks his wrist with an upward swing. "Bigger arc and a little more power next time."

I paste on a tired smile, and he pulls out the chair next to him. My uncle is a bean counter. He sits all day in an office counting beans or, in this case, taxpayer dollars for San Diego County. His office is a gray cubicle: gray carpet, gray walls, gray computer and desk. And he's surrounded by other gray cubicles filled with other people who get math and are more comfortable with numbers than words. Even his name has a gray quality. Bob.

But Uncle Bob has always supported me. He insisted I have Nova so I could have something of my mom. He's always been the quiet, stoic resident of the bungalow, but the look on his face after Pen knocked the time capsule to the floor killed me. He looked as broken as Pen's headless Polly Pocket doll.

"I'm sorry," I say. "I'm sorry I made a mess of things with

the time capsule and upset Pen. I'm sorry—"

Uncle Bob rests his hand on my fingers, which are plucking the woven threads on a rooster place mat. "It's okay." With his other hand, he reaches under the table and pulls out a metal box, the family time capsule. "This evening after the track meet, your aunt and I sat down and had a word with Penelope, and she told us about the list. As usual, Reb, I don't understand half the stuff you do, but I know that when you take something on, it's important to you, just like it was to your mother." He taps the top of the box, a metal *clank* filling the kitchen. "I got everything to fit, including your sea glass and jelly beans, and it's all sealed up."

I run my finger along the thick line of hardened glue sealing the time capsule, and a lump forms in my throat. Uncle Bob likes numbers and isn't good with words. That bead of glue around a metal box is his way of saying I'm a member of this family. That I belong here. I throw my arms around his neck and hug.

When I go to the room I share with Pen, the lights are out, but I can make out Penelope's form under the designer quilts. Her back is to me, her breath fast and uneven. I've shared a room with Pen for too many years not to know when she is faking sleep to avoid me.

Kicking aside the throw pillows scattered on the floor, I sit on the edge of my bed. "I'm sorry, Pen. I'm sorry I got disqualified from the track meet, and I'm sorry I made a mess of things with the time capsule. I'm sorry I hurt your feelings. Do you hear me? I'm sorry."

Pen says nothing. Maybe she'll never speak to me again. Maybe she'll hate me forever. Who knows? There's so much about this world we don't know. We can make choices, but they don't always go the way we plan.

At the end of the week, Macey and I head to the farmers' market after school. Today the market is crowded. Summer looms, and the bins are bursting. Long before we reach the fruit stalls, I smell the peaches, sweet and ripe, full of sunshine and sugar.

Macey picks out a half dozen plump peaches and pays.

"Is there an award winner in here?" I ask.

Macey's lips quirk. "Maybe." Macey's latest innovation is vodka in her pastry. Apparently when the pie bakes, the alcohol evaporates and the crust becomes light and flaky. She engineered a topping—sugar-dusted blueberries and dollops of whipped cream—that will be the perfect complement to the golden peaches. She held taste tests. She waited for the peaches to ripen. And she found makeup to cover her scars. Now is the time for the perfect peach pie.

And time to mend a screwed-up life. In the past month, I've managed to piss off my family, Nate's family, and the entire track-and-field team, all in my efforts to connect with others because I'm tired of being alone. Now it's time to put aside the list for a few days and try to mend fences.

On the way out of the market, we pass a citrus cart showcasing mountains of brilliant yellow, green, and orange. I stop and buy a dozen oranges so plump and bright, they look like tiny suns about to burst.

"So what will you do with all the money if you win the Great American Bake-Off?" I ask Macey as we leave the market.

Her bony shoulders shrug. "I haven't thought about it."

"A purist. You're in it for the pursuit of the perfect peach pie."

She pauses and ponders. "I guess so. Somewhere along the way this stopped being an assignment, and I started to care about pie."

"Wait a minute. What do you mean, this stopped being an assignment? You don't have a FACS class."

Macey unhooks her helmet—I now have two—but doesn't put it on. "You know that day we were in detention together, when Lungren made us write bucket lists?"

"That would be the day you bailed."

"I bailed from the room but not the assignment. Lungren wouldn't let me. You know how she is, thinking she can change lives and all? Anyway, she tracked me down after I left, and I kind of had a meltdown in her office, and when I scraped myself up off the floor, I found myself with a bucket list." She lifts the bag of peaches.

"One of your bucket-list items is to enter the Great American Bake-Off?"

"It's the only item on the list."

"Seriously?"

"I know, I'm not a normal person."

I toast her with my bag of oranges and toss them into Nova's basket.

After I drop Macey off at her house, I drive back to school. It's almost four o'clock, and the regional meet will start soon. I talked to the coach the day after I missed the qualifier. She didn't exactly kick me off the team, but she suggested that perhaps I might prefer tennis or golf. The track team doesn't need me, and while I don't need them, I failed them, and I need to make amends.

I park Nova in the lot near the track, smiling at the row of Red Rocket trees Percy and I planted. The manager at the plant store said these are fast-growing trees and in a few years will be providing shade to cars parked here for sporting events. Kennedy would approve.

Once I get to the track, I haul a five-gallon water jug to a small table near the benches for runners. I take another jug to the other set of benches near the field events, the seats where Pen and the Cupcakes sit, waiting for the meet to start.

Pen jumps from the bench. "What are you doing here?"

"Helping Liia set up."

"We don't need your help."

Ignoring the glare from Pen and perplexed frowns of the coaches, I fill water cups and cut oranges. A discus player from another team walks by my table. "Do you mind if I take a few orange slices?"

"Take ten, twenty. If you'd like, I can run to The Garden Spot and get you an entire tree."

The 100 Club project to enhance the nesting grounds for the California Least Terns, aka sea swallows, is done, and the birds have arrived. I have no reason to interact with Nate Bolivar, other than I miss him.

Yes, my shriveled little heart misses Nate. Of course I miss his kiss. I miss the dimples slashed across his cheeks, but most of all I miss being a couple, that feeling of being part of something bigger, something greater than myself. From Nate I learned that when you're a part of a couple or a family or a team, you sacrifice. You miss baseball practice so you can watch your brothers and sisters. You swing in the batting cages even though you're tired because it will help the team. You go to prom even if you're not a prom kind of girl because the guy you've fallen for is a prom kind of guy.

In biology I try to get Nate's attention, but he's too fascinated with Mr. Phillips's tie. After the final bell, I stop by Nate's desk. "Can we talk?"

"Nope." He makes a beeline for the door.

Even Mr. Phillips seems surprised by Nate's rudeness. "Problems with the sea swallow project, Rebecca?"

"No, we're done." With the project. But if I have my way, not with us.

After school I run to the baseball field. I immediately spot Nate talking to one of the coaches near the batting cage. Nate says something I can't hear. The coach throws up his hands and walks away, shaking his head. As Nate passes a five-gallon bucket of balls, he kicks the bucket. Balls spill across the ground.

I jog toward him, but Bronson, who's on the other side of the waist-high chain-link fence, catches my arm. "Leave him alone, Reb. He doesn't need anything from you right now."

I consider pulling away, but Bronson is one of Nate's best friends, and if I want a future with Nate, I have to make nice with Bronson. Not *nice* nice, but we need to get to the point where we're not tearing off each other's heads.

But I'm not good at small talk. "Why do you hate me?"

Bronson toes the turf. "It's not that I hate you, more like I don't get you." He wears cleats, good for digging in.

"But you get that I like Nate, right?"

The bald patch of dirt grows.

"Listen, Bronson, I need to talk to Nate."

"You hurt him once already. I'm not going to let you do it again."

"You think I like seeing him that way?" I rest my hands on the top of the fence.

"I have no idea what you think. Like I said, I don't get you, and I don't like what's happened to my best friend."

The metal of the fence digs into my palms. "Which is why I need to talk to him. Something's wrong. He's skipping practice, and you have a game tomorrow." I know because I checked the sports calendar on the school website. Being the other half of a couple with a sporto means parking my butt in the bleachers and shaking a pom-pom.

"Nate quit the team."

I suck in a fast breath. He finally admitted the truth and made a choice. A part of me celebrates Nate's decision, but I worry about him, because he's dealing with fallout that often comes when you blast your own course. "Help me, Bronson. How can I reach him?"

Bronson stops kicking the helpless grass and jogs away from the field.

I hurry along my side of the fence. "Doesn't it make sense that if I broke everything, I can try to fix it?" Or make a fool of myself trying. He keeps jogging, and by the time we reach the men's locker room, I have no more words, no more arguments.

Bronson walks by me toward the door, mumbling something that sounds like *My barber is kind of grungy* or *Try the harbor on Sunday.*

When I get to the harbor late Sunday morning, I go straight to the kayak rental shop. Since the storm a few days ago, we've had smooth waters and buckets of sunshine. The shop owner tells me I can find Nate at a bay of kayaks near the loading beach. When I arrive, Nate's standing at the water's edge with an older couple, showing them how to paddle. His skin has soaked up more sun and is a deeper bronze. He wears a white tank, knee-length surf shorts, and no shoes.

After the paddling lessons, Nate jogs to a trailer of kayaks. I could watch Nate all day, but that would get me no closer to prom.

My bare toes digging into the sand, I join Nate at the trailer. "We need to talk."

"I'm working." Which means he can't bail on me.

Thank you, Bronson, thank you. "I'm sorry I called you a liar."

Nate unfastens the straps anchoring a kayak to the trailer. "You were being honest. I'm not living my own life, not being true to myself. I—"

"But—"

"—can't tell people no." He lugs the kayak onto the sand. "I lied to myself that I want to play baseball and run for class president. I lied about wanting to get my MBA."

"But I didn't have to say it the way I said it."

"Sometimes people need a good slam upside the head." He wraps the kayak strap around his wrist. "Gets them out of bad situations."

"So I'm a bad situation?"

"There is no situation. There is no us." Yanking on the strap, he drags the boat through the sand.

I follow him. The older couple stands at the end of the loading ramp in plastic spray skirts that remind me of oval tutus. *Excuse me, Grandma and Gramps, but can you please go pirouette elsewhere so I can grovel without an audience?* They don't budge.

"Nate, you're a good guy."

He drags the kayak to the edge of the loading ramp.

"I was an idiot not to hold your hand in public."

He takes the paddles from Grandma and Gramps and sets them on the concrete ramp.

"And not to accept your offer to go to prom."

Taking a towel from his waist, he wipes the sand off the seats.

"And a hundred other things in the How-to-Screw-Up-a-Relationship Handbook."

The older couple stares from me to Nate, as if we're playing tennis.

"So what I'm trying to say is," I continue, "would you go to prom with me?"

The waves lap against the kayak. The old couple inches closer.

"Come on, Nate, say something. Or tell me why you're avoiding me. I deserve that."

Nate looks at the sky. "You're complicated."

"You don't like complicated?"

"No. Yes." He runs a hand through the sides of his hair. "The problem is, my life got complicated."

"Because of me?"

"No, because of me, but technically, you're involved. You made me look at who I was and what I wanted, and you know what? I stared into the mirror and saw quite a bit I didn't like. That made me angry."

"And there's always something under the anger."

"What?" Nate asks. He helps the older woman into the kayak and clips her spray skirt to the seat opening.

"Pie therapy," I say. "There's something under the crust, something more substantial. So you're more than angry."

The older man steps into the kayak, and Nate clips his spray skirt into place. "The truth," Nate says, "is that it scared the hell out of me. Do you remember Herman the shark from Mr. Phillips's biology lecture, the one that didn't move out of a ten-foot space even though he had an Olympic-size pool?" He jabs his chest with his fingertips, the movements hard and jerky. "I'm Herman. I'm. Herman." His hands fall limply at his sides. "For years I've had my life planned, and everything within that little box has been fine. Baseball scholarship, undergrad work at a major university, business school, which at one point is what I wanted, but somewhere along the way, I stopped wanting that."

"People change. Dreams and plans need to change, too."

"Tell that to my parents and baseball coach, or to Gabby, who I was going to send to fashion-design school, or Marco, who I was going to send to the seminary." He runs a weary hand down his face.

"Something tells me you already have told them."

"Yeah. Didn't go over too well."

Hope sparks deep in my gut. "So it can't get much worse from here. Go to prom with me."

Nate's eyelids plunk closed, as if he's too tired to take on the arduous being that is me.

"Go to prom with her, dear," Grandma says.

"She seems like a nice little gal," Gramps adds.

Nate finally opens his eyes. "I can't. I'm going with a girl from my calculus class."

19. Learn math

CHAPTER
TWENTY

AS I'VE LEARNED FROM BOTH PERCY AND AUNT Evelyn, when life gets messy, you need blue cleaning products. I'm not sure why that makes me laugh, but it does. Swallowing a giggle, I carry Aunt Evelyn's cleaning basket from the laundry room to my bedroom. Nothing should be very funny right now. I dug into the deepest part of my heart, carved out a chunk, and gave it to Nate. Nate, however, is going to prom with someone else, a girl from his calculus class.

Ouch.

Once in my bedroom, I have no idea where to start. I've heard of hoarders, people who acquire things and can't give them away. Some compulsive hoarders have so much stuff, they live in homes with little pathways winding through piles of clutter. I'm not a hoarder; more of an annoyer. Someone like Macey's therapist would have a technical name for this condition. For years I amassed stuff on my side of the room because it annoyed Aunt Evelyn and Cousin Pen. The truth is, it also annoys me. Nate isn't the only one who's been lying to himself.

I start with the floor, folding and putting away clean laundry. I gather all my color-coordinated pillows and arrange them, or at least I try to. The jumble of pillows looks like the pillow fairy barfed on my bed.

"What are you doing?" Pen stands in the doorway with a frown.

"Cleaning," I say.

"Why?"

"My side of the room's a mess."

"You just had this epiphany?"

"No. Yes." Next I start scooping up papers: school reports, homework assignments, old sketches and drawings. "Don't make this any more complicated than it needs to be."

"You're the one who complicates things."

"I know." I toss papers into the wastebasket next to my desk until it overflows. "I remember what you said. Your parents never fought before I came to live in the bungalow."

"And this could be some part of your master plan to pit my dad against my mom."

I reach for the wastebasket near Penelope's desk. "Or not."

Pen snatches it back and places it on her side of the room before stomping out the door.

"Hey! I'm trying to do good!"

With the floor clean, I dust furniture, wall hangings, and the glass jars sitting on the windowsill. I spray blue stuff on the window and mirror and scrub. As the dust and grime wash away, I feel light-headed. I wonder if Aunt Evelyn gets a cleaning high or if it's the blue products. When everything else is clean, I dig out the stuff under my bed.

It's funny the things that accumulate under one's bed over time: dust bunnies, a half stick of deodorant, a single soccer cleat, a person's past. Aunt Evelyn loves boxes, especially stackable plastic boxes you can tuck under beds. The one storage box under my bed is twenty-four by eighteen inches with a red lid. It doesn't look like a coffin, but inside rests everything that's left of my mom.

I hook my fingers around the latches but don't open. My mom never had much. Travel Light types rarely do. She never owned a house, never rented a storage shed, and most of her stuff burned in the car crash.

Slowly, I slide off the lid. My mom's past smells like sky and smoke.

Inside there's a camera and a few lenses, her favorite denim jacket, and a tiny charm bracelet with a single daisy. At the bottom lies a large manila envelope. This doesn't belong to Mom but to me. Six years ago, I made the choice to tuck it out of sight.

My fingers settle on the bulge in the center of the envelope. Choices. We all make them. My mom didn't choose to die, but she did choose to drive on that road, one of the most dangerous in the world, in a rainstorm. She wanted to get post-storm pictures high on the mountain. She wanted to capture light and rainbows and slivers of silver peeking from retreating clouds. She should have waited. If I had been able to talk about my feelings after her death, I would have told Aunt Evelyn I was angry at Mom for leaving me and, underneath that, frightened. I wasn't ready for her death; I wasn't ready for the rest of the world.

I tip the envelope, and photos tumble into my lap. Mom was a photographer, and I was her favorite subject. Photos of me smiling, posing at a Mayan pyramid and sitting on the beach in Costa Rica, spill across my clean floor. There are close-ups of my face, artistic shots of me in silhouette, pictures of my dirty toes. I dig through me until I find her. My mom rarely stepped in front of the camera. I snapped this photo a few months before she died. She's sitting on the side of a mountain road in Argentina fixing a flat tire on the Jeep, sweaty, dirty, and smiling from ear to ear.

"She looks happy." I look up to see Aunt Evelyn standing in my doorway. Other than perfunctory hellos and *Please pass the salt*, we've talked very little this week. "Your mom's happy place was always outdoors, on the beach, high on a mountain, or in a field of daisies under the open sky." She points at the photo. "May I?" She takes the photo and tilts her head, the football helmet shifting. "It's a good one. It would look great in one of your picture frames."

For six years I kept all reminders of my mother packed away because I didn't want to be reminded of what I was missing. Family. "I was thinking about using the frame with the daisies or the one with the clouds."

Aunt Evelyn hands me back the photo. "Either would look lovely. You are a good artist, Rebel. I bet I could sell the frames for twenty or thirty dollars apiece to my clients with beach houses."

"That would buy some serious turtle adoptions."

"Excuse me?"

"Nothing." I take comfort in The List, because Macey's right. I haven't failed at *everything*. And Nate and Uncle Bob are right. I'll complete every item because I said I would. There's no deadline, after all. As long as I keep trying.

Aunt Evelyn sits on the window seat and slides her finger along the lip of a jar of sea glass. "I envy you." She scoops a handful of glass into her palm and lets the shards fall back into the jar, a shower of sea tears. "When I was in high school, I desperately wanted to be an artist. I worked in watercolors and did some graphite sketches. One of my art teachers said I had an excellent handle on perspective and a good eye for composition. What I didn't have was passion or faith."

The last word hangs in the air between us.

"Now your mother, she had faith."

"My mother didn't believe in God."

"No, but she had faith in herself. She barreled through life with passion and purpose, and she was a damned good photographer. Her work told stories; it spoke to people."

I've never heard Aunt Evelyn talk this way about my mom. She was always so critical of Mom and her parenting style, but it's true. My mom had faith in her photographic talents. She had faith in her abilities to be a single parent. She had faith in me that I could lead my own 275-member marching band.

"You have her spirit, her passion, her unwavering faith." The final bit of glass slips between my aunt's fingers. "I don't have that. I never did. So instead of creating art, I create pretty rooms in pretty houses." She raises her hands, motioning to the matched twin beds. "But you'll never find yourself doing anything like this. I envy you, Rebel, because you will never work or live inside a box."

Breakfast the next morning is a mushroom quiche and grapefruit juice, fresh-squeezed. Aunt Evelyn stands at the counter toasting brioche. She doesn't mention our little heart-to-heart. I don't, either. But she looks different, or maybe it's that I'm seeing her differently. Tiny lines spider out from her mouth. The skin under her eyes swells in puffs of gray. She doesn't look unhappy, more resigned about her life and the choices she made.

Outside, the recycling truck lumbers and lurches. A steady beep fills the air as the arm lifts our bin and dumps the contents. My life would have been so different if a month ago Uncle Bob had chosen to set out the recycling bin and this truck had whisked away Kennedy's bucket list. I wouldn't realize Aunt Evelyn is a frustrated artist and that I'm tired of being a loner.

The list. Such a flimsy piece of paper with so much power to change, and I'm not even done. I've completed about half the items, but I still have—

I set my juice down so hard, liquid sunshine spills over the rim.

"Is there something wrong with your breakfast?" Aunt Evelyn asks.

I run to my room and shuffle through my nightstand drawer. I check under the bed and rifle through my dresser. I tear open the closet door and toss aside my shoes and Pen's shoes and little boxes that organize.

"Where is it?" I say. I didn't see Kennedy's bucket list during my cleaning tirade yesterday. I press my hands to either side of my head.

I haven't seen the list in a week, sometime before the day I failed to Just Show Up, the day Gabby burned off half her hair, and the day I threw muddy shoes at endangered sea swallows.

I'd last seen the list on my nightstand. I pull the heavy piece of furniture from the wall, and the lamp topples to the hardwood floor with a thud. Behind it I find only a gum wrapper and a few popcorn kernels.

In the attic, I dig through my sketch pads and check behind jars of glass. Downstairs I root under the couch and toss aside throw pillows. I dig through the kitchen garbage and nooks and crannies on the computer desk. When I get to the empty recycling bin, I remember pitching all the papers and junk from my cleaning tirade yesterday.

"No." My voice is a squeak.

At school I rummage through my locker, pulling out books and half-used sketch pads and a pink detention slip from October.

"What are you doing?" Macey asks.

"I can't find Kennedy's bucket list. It's gone. I checked every room in our house."

Macey leans against the locker next to mine. "Maybe the fates have intervened again."

I stick my fingers into my ears. "La-la-la-la. I can't hear you."

Macey tugs my fingers from my ears. "I think you need to hear me."

"I need to get to biology."

"Stop being a smart-ass." Macey is so loud, a teacher at the end of the hall makes a *shush* motion with her forefinger against her lips. "Think about it, Rebel. For days you tried to get rid of that list, and you couldn't. So you decided to complete the tasks. Maybe you've completed the task or tasks you needed to complete, so the fates have released you."

"Stop. No more."

"Maybe it's destiny."

"La-la-la-la-laaaaaa!"

Every morning the sun pours buckets of light onto a three-foot square of earth on the east side of the bungalow. This tiny bit of real estate is nestled between the recycling bin and the large plastic storage cupboard where Aunt Evelyn keeps most of her gardening supplies. Aunt Evelyn never planted anything here, probably because no one sees it.

Which makes it the perfect place for a secret garden.

I checked my locker at school and the art room. I checked Percy's office. Aunt Evelyn and I turned the house upside down. I can't find Kennedy's bucket list, but I do remember she wrote twenty items on the list, and so far I've remembered seventeen, including *Host a tea party in a secret garden.*

With all my strength, I harpoon the shovel at the earth. The metal clanks and chips off a sliver of hard dirt. Thanks to running, my legs are strong. With my sneakered foot, I stomp on the shovel, and a bigger chunk of baked earth breaks off. I jab the tip on the clod until it forms medium-size clods. I stomp and jab, jab and stomp. Sweat beads on my forehead and drips down my nose.

A wet nose nuzzles my ankle. Tiberius, the rat terrier from next door, stands next to me, wagging his tail. "Sorry, Tib, no sweets for you today." He cocks his head and thumps his butt onto the ground.

I grab a pronged gardening tool and drop to my hands and knees, clawing at the ground to break the medium-size clods into smaller clods. Tiberius watches, his ratty head tilted as if he is confused. I'm not sure if it's because I don't toss him something to eat or because I'm engaging in hand-to-hand combat with dirt.

Less than halfway through the square, sweat soaks my tank, and silty dust coats my arms and legs. There must be an easier way to battle rock-hard dirt. I sit on the backs of my ankles and wipe sweat from my face. Water. If seawater has the power to smooth jagged glass, surely water can soften a secret garden.

With the hose in hand, I spray the plot of earth, transforming the dirt into chunks of dark chocolate. I shovel, but the mud is heavy and clings to the metal. My arm muscles burn. I could get Macey, but then the secret garden would cease to be a secret. Taking off my shoes, I roll up my pants and jump. Mud squishes between my toes and sucks at my calves. I march and squish.

When at last the entire plot is soaked, I climb out, scraping the mud from my legs. I reach for my box of seeds, but they're gone. Tiberius sits near my bag, two seed packets, empty but for teeth marks, between his paws.

"You ate my seeds."

He nuzzles my hand.

"You ate my seeds!" Mud covers every inch of skin to my knees. Speckles of brown dot my shirt, my face, my hair. "This is so wrong." I settle my back against the recycling bin and slide to the ground. Tiberius lies next to me. "Or maybe it's fate." I scratch Tiberius's head, and he closes his eyes. "Maybe you ate the seeds because I'm not meant to plant those seeds. Instead of daisies, maybe I'm supposed to plant petunias or snapdragons."

Now my brain hurts.

"Or maybe this is a sign that I'm supposed to make another choice. Maybe it's time to give up the whole thing." But I'm not ready to give up Kennedy's list. The list brought me Nate, and it brought me closer to Macey and Percy and Uncle Bob and Aunt Evelyn.

Of course I could always perform the acts on my own list. I laugh so loudly, Tiberius cracks an eyelid. I hadn't taken the assignment seriously, not like Kennedy and Macey. I wrote about surfing naked and riding in a shopping cart yelling, "The British are coming! The British are coming!" The detention assignment was a joke. I wiggle my toes, clumps of mud falling to the ground.

Well, not all of it was a joke.

Like Kennedy, I'd written a page of bucket-list items. But it was only in those final minutes in the detention room when I'd been thinking about death and dying and heaven that I dug into my heart. The last two items on my list were very much about connecting with others.

What now, Kennedy? You love to talk and haven't been shy about sharing advice before.

Silence.

I'm waiting.

More silence. I toe the mud on the top of my foot. It's been days since I've heard her voice—not since that day at the mudflats when I welcomed the sea swallows and swore at her. If people and situations are truly put into our lives when we need them, is it possible I just don't need Kennedy anymore? An uncomfortable shiver rocks my spine. I turn to the sky and hear only birds and the far-off crash of the ocean.

"What do you think, Tib? Is it time to give up the bone?"

Tiberius snores.

I picture those final two items, two lines faintly scratched, two lines that caused an unexpected ache in the center of my chest. I pretended they didn't matter, and I quickly tossed those words into the trash. But as I think of those two lines now, I realize they do matter. With Kennedy's list gone, mine is the only one I have left.

With the hose, I wash my feet and take the first steps toward completing my bucket list.

20. Find my father

CHAPTER
TWENTY-ONE

I AIM MY PENCIL STUB LIKE A PISTOL AT MY notebook. *Find My Father* sounds way too normal. I lick the tip of my pencil and write, Yo, Dad, Where are you?

1. Name: Antoine
2. Occupation: French Canadian journalist
3. Interests: art, art museums, South America
4. Last known whereabouts: Buenos Aires, Argentina
5. Physical: eyes the color of milk chocolate with a dash of nutmeg
6. ???

That's it. Five pathetic lines. All I know about my father. All my mother knew about him. They'd both been on assignment in Buenos Aires, the Paris of South America. My father was covering some art installation, and Mom was shooting the Iguazu Falls. She called my father the Gift Giver. "Because he gave me the best gift of my entire life. You."

Growing up, I occasionally wondered about him. Was he an artist? Was he short? Did he hate shoes? After my mom's death, when it became clear I didn't belong in the bungalow, I imagined running away and finding my father. As with Mom, we'd travel the world, and I'd tag along on his assignments. I'd shake hands with world-famous artists, and we'd talk about color and composition. On my imaginary dad's days off, we'd explore the world's finest museums and hunt for shark teeth.

I'm curious about my father and figure he must be quite extraordinary for my mom to have taken an interest in him. When Uncle Bob and Aunt Evelyn get home, I'll ask them about him. I'll also try to track down some of my mom's journalist friends and see if they know anything. And if I'm really desperate, I can thumb through art magazines and newspapers to track down journalists writing about museums in Buenos Aires the year I was born.

The world feels so big.

When Penelope gets home, I join her at the kitchen table to start on the final item on my bucket list. Taking a deep breath,

I hand Cousin Pen a bag from Target, the plastic crinkling and crunching.

"What's this?" Pen holds the bag far from her body, as if something alive lurks inside and might bite.

I lounge with one elbow resting on the kitchen counter, trying to appear relaxed, trying to pretend that what I'm about to ask isn't gnawing at my gut. "Something for you. A present."

She shakes it and sniffs.

"Come on, Pen. Open the stupid bag."

My cousin pushes aside her calc book, sets the bag on the table, and reaches in, but her hand freezes.

I leap across the kitchen, pull out the box, and set the Polly Pocket doll directly in front of her. "It's supposed to be a bribe."

"Supposed to be?"

I plunk onto the chair next to Pen. "I went to the store to buy you something that would bring you great joy and give you warm, fuzzy feelings for me so you'd do me a favor."

"And this is what you came up with?"

"It made sense at the time."

"Really?"

"Really." I jam my hands through my hair. "So I'm walking down an aisle at Target and see this display of Polly Pockets. The display includes cars and bakeries and pet shops. Then I see you and your friends. I see you playing with the dolls and all the little things that go with them. You used to make up these elaborate games and stories." I rake my fingers down the back of my skull to my neck. "Then I see me. I'm sitting on my bed and watching you all, and I remember feeling hurt that no one invited me to play. And then I thought of pie."

"Rebel, you are so screwed up."

"I know, but at least I know why. When I broke the heads off your Polly Pocket dolls, everyone, including me, thought I was angry because you threw away all my sea glass. But I don't have attachments to things, because *things* aren't important to me. I wasn't angered by the missing glass. I was hurt because you and your friends were ignoring me. I wanted to be part of your game."

Pen studies the front of the box, the back of the box, and both sides of the box.

"Yeah, it's getting deep," I say. "So let's both forget about my epiphany in the Target toy aisle and think of the doll as a bribe."

Pen sets the doll on her math book and leans back in her chair. "Spill. What do you want?"

"I need a prom ticket."

The front legs of Pen's chair clatter to the floor, and she looks relieved. "Impossible. Prom is this Saturday. The committee isn't selling tickets anymore."

"I know, but I figured at least one of the Cupcakes is on the prom committee."

Pen tilts her head. "So if you need a prom ticket, is it correct to assume that you'll be going to prom?"

"Yes."

"And if you're going to prom, is it correct to assume you may act in a manner that is far from normal?"

"Yes."

Pen presses her palms to the sides of her head, as if she's trying to keep it from exploding. "Is this about Kennedy Green's bucket list?"

"No."

Pen's stare sharpens.

I tilt my chair back, wobble, and settle all four legs back on the floor. "It's about *my* bucket list."

She laughs so hard, her ponytail swings. "One of the items on your bucket list is 'Go to prom'?"

"Not exactly."

She drums her fingers on the table. I sit patiently, thinking of peaches.

"And if I don't get you a ticket?" Penelope asks.

"I'll crash prom."

"Why do I not doubt that?" Pen sighs and pulls her cell phone from her pocket. "Let me talk to Sandy. She's on the committee."

The next day after school Macey stands in her tiny kitchen in the FACS building while a member of the school newspaper takes her picture. She's holding a green ribbon with gold lettering in one hand, a peach pie in the other.

The newspaper staffer settles her camera around her neck and takes out a long, skinny notepad from the back pocket of her shorts. "Are you disappointed you didn't win the local round of the Great American Bake-Off?"

Macey tosses the ribbon onto the counter. "Of course not."

"But you didn't win any prize money and didn't move on to the next round."

"My goal wasn't to win the bake-off, just enter it."

Now the staffer looks confused. "So you're happy with a ribbon of participation?"

"I'm happy with my pie." Macey hands the newspaper photographer the pie and shoos her out of the FACS kitchen.

I sit on the counter, my flip-flops tapping the cupboard. Raising my hand, I make a giant check mark in the air. "Bucket list complete. Congratulations."

Macey pulls me off the counter. "Now time for yours."

Together Macey and I drive to the Bolivar house. When Gabby opens the door and sees me, her eyes grow wide but quickly narrow into a glare. She jams her arms over her chest, her new, sleek haircut swinging. The hair hangs to her chin at the sides and is cut short at the back. She wears vampy bangs slashed with a streak of hot pink.

"Good choice," I say. "Pink's a great color on you."

Gabby wrinkles her nose. "It's the clip-on kind."

"Even so, it has panache."

Her teeth dig into her bottom lip. "You think so?"

"I know so." I squat and grab her hands. "So much that I'm here on my knees begging for your help."

"My help?"

"I need a prom dress, something with massive amounts of panache, and I only have forty bucks and two days."

Gabby's jaw drops. "Two days is not a lot of time to find a prom dress."

"I know."

"This time of year, dresses have been picked over."

"I know."

Her expression grows grimmer. "And it'll be hard to find a dress for forty dollars."

"I know." I grab her hand. "Which is why I need you."

Gabby turns her face skyward as if seeking help from every god in the universe to deal with me. Then she peeks at me out of the corner of her eye to make sure I'm watching this show of diva drama. "This is not going to be easy."

"I know."

She pulls herself so close, our noses almost touch. "But I like you, Rebel."

"I know."

Gabby squeezes my hand and runs through the entryway, calling over her shoulder, "Okay, get in here. We have a lot of work to do."

Next to me, Macey lowers her head. "She scares me."

"But she has panache," I say.

We follow Gabby into the living room. "You know, if you would have given me two weeks, I could have made something."

"And it would have been spectacular and unique and perfect for me."

"But we don't have two weeks." Gabby pushes up her sleeves and points to a stack of fashion magazines. "Start flipping through those, and let me know what you like."

For the next half hour Macey and I go through Gabby's fashion magazines while Gabby holds color swatches to my face and makes dire clucking sounds.

"Look at this one," I say as I point to a bright purple dress with puffy tiers. "I like the color."

"Too much ruching," Gabby says. "Not good for short people like you. You'd look like a gnome."

I point to a sheath in pale yellow. "This one's less poufy. Plus, I like the small straps."

"Wrong color. You'd look like a seasick caterpillar."

"Gabby, you know, this isn't good for my fragile ego," I say with more than a hint of truth.

"We don't have time for egos." She holds her hand out to Macey. "Hand me the next stack of color swatches."

"Maybe I should wear cargo pants and a tank."

Macey and Gabby don't laugh.

"That was a joke." I thought prom was supposed to be fun. It's starting to scare me.

Once Gabby is armed with ideas and colors, we head for the mall. None of the dresses are right. One dress, a light blue thing with a petallike skirt, is doable but four times my budget. I sold two of my frames to Aunt Evelyn for one of her staged beach houses, and I have exactly forty dollars, but Gabby is determined. After coming up empty at the mall, we head to a thrift store off Calle Bonita, where we find plenty of eighties-type prom dresses with big sleeves and butt bows.

Macey digs through a rack and finds a bright blue slinky dress with a single shoulder strap and wispy train. "What do you think of this one?"

"I'd get tangled in the skirt, fall, and make an even bigger fool of myself," I say.

"Definitely not for you," Gabby says. "But *you* could pull it off, Macey."

"I don't wear colors," Macey says.

"Maybe you should," Gabby says as she browses through the rack. "That will look drop-dead gorgeous on you."

"Yeah, Macey, try it on. That way you can be my date."

Macey realizes I'm not joking. She tugs at her hoodie sleeve. "I can't, Rebel."

I don't press her. Some things take time, like peaches. "Maybe after a few more pies."

Macey puts the dress back on the rack. "Maybe."

I try on more than twenty dresses. Nothing fits. Nothing looks good. Nothing is right. The only thing that piques

Gabby's interest is a slim, floor-length, whitish dress with thin straps and a wispy overskirt, but it has a stain the shape of the Hawaiian Islands on the front.

"Maybe it's a sign." I hang the dress back on the rack and puff back the lock of sweaty hair dangling over my forehead. "Maybe I'm not meant to go to prom."

"No," Macey and Gabby say in unison. Gabby hands me the stained dress. "Try it on."

I slip on the dress and walk out of the tiny dressing room stall. "It's . . ."

". . . plain," Macey finishes for me.

"There's no color, no flair," I say. Nothing screams *I'm different and proud of it*. The dress isn't pure white, more like ivory, and the overskirt is delicate and gauzy. It has a high waist and narrow skirt, something that might have been worn to a wedding in the 1960s. "And it's too long. Plus, there's Hawaii."

A glint fires in Gabby's eyes. "But it has panache."

21. Fall in love

CHAPTER
TWENTY-TWO

"YOU HAVE A ZIT!" GABBY PRESSES HER HANDS TO her cheeks.

"It's not the end of the world." Macey pushes me onto the edge of my bed and takes a cosmetics bag from her purse. "I have a great concealer."

I hug a throw pillow to my chest. "Maybe it is the end of the world. So let's forget about prom and hang out and make s'mores."

Gabby gives me a don't-even-go-there look.

Macey smooths lotion over my face and neck. Then she dots concealer onto my chin, covering the lone pimple that had the nerve to show up on the day of what will most likely be my one and only prom. With sure, steady hands, Macey blends the edges and smooths on a thin layer of foundation.

"Been practicing?" I ask.

"A little." She dusts my entire face with a light coating of powder. "An extraordinary person once told me a bit of cover-up doesn't change who you are on the inside, just hides some things that distract others from seeing what's important."

I breathe in the pie wisdom. I'm falling for Nate, and, for him, I'm choosing to go to prom.

Macey applies a touch of eyeliner, mascara, and only traces of blush and lip gloss. "Gabby says less is more."

"Glad one of us has a handle on things," I mutter. My fingers pluck at the throw pillow.

One of the Cupcakes, a girl named Sandy, walks in, and Gabby squeals with too much joy. "Hair time! I want a half-up, half-down, with curls framing her face."

Sandy is a Cupcake. She is also one of my dates. The Cupcakes, those who don't have couple-type dates, are in Aunt Evelyn and Uncle Bob's master bedroom and bathroom primping and preening for prom. Last night when Pen invited me to go to prom with her and her friends, my jaw fell to the floor.

"Why are you asking me?" I'd said. One Polly Pocket does not a relationship make.

Pen's lips had pinched below her wrinkled-up nose. "I have no choice."

"Aunt Evelyn's making you?"

"Sucks to be me," Pen said, but the words lacked her normal bite. While Pen and I still aren't bosom buddies, I accepted the date. Walking into prom on the arm of a Cupcake is better than walking into prom alone.

The Cupcake hairdresser pulls my hair into a tight upsweep. My eyes stretch and tilt, and my temples throb. "Feels a little tight," I say.

She smooths loose curls along my shoulders. "You can't have it too loose, or the hair will fall out of the updo while you're dancing."

I'm not sure if tonight's mission will include dancing. There are no formulas, mathematic or otherwise, on how to take the guy you're falling in love with from a girl in his calc class. I can tap his date's shoulder and say *Excuse me, but may I cut in?*

Or . . . *Back away from the sporto, Calculus Girl; he's mine.*

Or . . . *Choose me.*

I nibble the inside of my cheek while the Cupcake spritzes my head with hair spray and proclaims me done.

"Now for the dress." Gabby wiggles her fingers in excitement and pulls the plastic from a dress hanging on the back of my door. If there is a God—and the jury's still out on that—he or she is yukking it up with a choir of heavenly angels at the idea of me owning and *wearing* a prom dress.

Macey helps Gabby slip the gown over my head, and I try not to panic as the gauzy fabric flutters down my body. The dress no longer looks like a 1960s bridesmaid dress. Gabby shortened the front to thigh length, and soft folds of ivory taper at the sides and hang to the floor in the back. She pulls a wide, light blue velvet ribbon from her fairy-godmother bag and ties it under my bustline, hiding Hawaii. The band of high-waisted color makes me look taller, and in some magical illusion, more full-chested.

"Now this." With a flourish, Gabby pulls a hair clip from her bag.

I run my fingers over colorful glass. "It's beautiful. Where'd you find it?"

"Your aunt made it," Gabby says. "I called her to get some sea glass because I was thinking about gluing it to a barrette, but she offered to make something instead."

Gabby clips on the ivory barrette, and bits of blue, frosty glass hang in a sparkly wing along one side of my face. My aunt is staging my hair. I should laugh, but I'm too nervous.

Gabby runs into the hallway like an excited puppy and calls out, "Pen, you got the box?"

Penelope carries in a shoe box and eyes me from head to toe, grimacing only slightly. At least she didn't make gagging sounds. "Here. I wore them last year to the Mistletoe Ball."

Macey pulls a pair of gargantuan heels from the box. They're ivory stilettos with pearls and scalloped lace along the sides. Gabby clasps her hands to her chest. "Oh, Penelope. These are perfect. She'll look like a frosty mermaid."

Gabby's right. The flowing ivory gown, blue swirling ribbon, wave of shimmering blue sea glass, and sparkly shoes are perfect. "Except for one little problem," I point out. "I'll break my leg after ten steps."

"You've tangoed in heels," Gabby reminds me. But that was when Nate the Great stood at my side. It's easy to dance in heels when you know someone's there to catch you when you fall.

"Can't you at least try?" Gabby is no longer the demanding fashion diva. She looks like a little girl caught playing in her mother's closet who's been told the game of dress-up is over.

I grab the daggerlike shoes and try not to growl. "Okay."

"Time to go!" Uncle Bob yells from the living room.

Macey offers me her arm, and I hobble out of the bungalow. In the front yard, Aunt Evelyn poses us on the porch in front of flowers and under a lattice arch while Uncle Bob takes photos. I try to duck behind a giant flowerpot, but Aunt Evelyn drags me into the picture.

"The corsage!" Gabby screams as we're walking down the path. "I forgot the corsage."

Cousin Pen groans, and Aunt Evelyn looks panicky. Uncle Bob walks across the porch and plucks a spray of small white flowers from one of the giant flowerpots. Daisies. My mom's favorite flower. With a wink, he hands me the flowers, which I tuck into the blue velvet ribbon above my waist.

Gabby claps her hands in approval and gives me a hug. "Have a magical time."

I squeeze back, not with as much joy as Gabby, but with sincerity and gratefulness. I know nothing of this world, and it scares the hell out of me. Only for Nate would I be something I'm not. When you care for someone, you sacrifice. At least for one night.

Pen and the Cupcakes walk toward the car while Macey gives my hand a final squeeze. "Good luck." Her tone is grave but fused with steel, as if she's sending me off to battle. I picture land mines and bombs and smoking guns. I squeeze Macey's hand and head for the car. I make it two steps when I spin and run back into the house.

"Noooooooooooo!" Gabby runs after me.

I wave her off. "It's okay. I'll be back. I need to get something."

Pen grumbles, and the look on her face asks *Causing trouble already, are we?*

I hurry to my room, now quiet and filled with fading light. I open my nightstand drawer and slide my hand along the bottom, fumbling through the clutter until I find the penny. My prom dress has no pockets, and Gabby didn't have time to find or manufacture a matching purse. I tear a single stitch from the skirt hem. Loosening a few more stitches, I slip in Percy's wheat penny, the one that saved his life.

Percy believes in lucky pennies, Macey believes in forces to combat evil, Kennedy believes in higher beings, and Nate believes in God and His saintly army. I'm still not ready to admit that something else may have a hand in my destiny, but tonight I'll take all the help I can get.

I sit in the backseat of a Cupcake-mobile.

I giggle at the thought. The other girls in the backseat sniff. They must think I'm drunk. I press my lips together, holding in maniacal laughter—and the contents of my stomach. By the time we get to the Del Rey Nature Preserve, this year's prom venue, my head feels as if someone buried an ax in my scalp.

"You guys go ahead and go in," I tell the Cupcakes as we pile out of the car. "I need to fix this hair-clip thingy."

"You sure?" Sandy asks. "It might be awkward to walk in by yourself. We can wait."

Three other Cupcakes nod. Even Pen gives me a quick dip.

"Go ahead," I insist. "I'll only be a minute."

Pen shuts the car door but doesn't leave my side. "You okay?"

I slide my fingers into the hair shellacked to the side of my head and try to tug loose a few hairs. "No."

"Do you want to go home?"

"No, I need to do this." Or I will regret with every cell in my body not trying to patch things up with Nate. I want him to know I'm willing to do this. For him.

"Then stop messing with your hair. You're going to ruin your look." Penelope untangles my fingers and tugs a lock from the updo. "There, that's better."

The skin at my temples is less tight, and my head no longer

throbs. Pen holds a compact mirror. A long blue streak spirals down one side of my face. Much better. I steady my hands on the sides of my gown. I have nothing to lose tonight. Nate's already not talking to me, and I don't give a crap about embarrassing myself in front of Del Rey School luminaries. I can do this.

A pathway of crisscrossing bricks leads to the entrance of the preserve's event center. My step grows steady and quickens. When Pen and I reach the entryway, I lift my foot to the first step, but I can't move. I give my foot a tug and stumble forward. Pen grabs me before my carefully made-up face slams into the sandstone patio.

"I told Gabby I can't walk in heels," I say.

Pen helps me stand upright, but I fall again. I look at my foot and see half a shoe. The stiletto heel is wedged between two bricks. I reach down and snatch the broken heel from the ground and slip out of the shoes.

Pen gasps. "You are not walking in there barefoot, are you?"

"I don't have much of a choice," I say on a hiss.

Pen rubs her knuckle across her chin. "I guess you're right. Everyone takes their shoes off after pictures anyway."

I breathe in her words. Right here, right now, bare feet are right. The sandstone is gritty but still warm from the sun. My mom didn't sign me up for soccer or dance lessons, and she was a horrible math teacher, but she taught me how to be confident in bare feet. Anyway, Nate likes my toes, and according to his ten-year-old sister, he *like* likes me.

With the wounded pair of shoes dangling from my finger-tips, I walk into prom with Pen. The sign on the easel at the door announces *Welcome to Bella Notte.*

Before me stretches an Italian courtyard. Roman columns guard the entryway. Trellises with grapevines line the walls. Twinkle lights hang from potted trees. At the photo station sits a gondola against the backdrop of a faded Venetian palazzo.

Ride in a gondola in Venice, Italy, with the love of my life.

I get dizzy, and Pen jumps back. "Do not throw up on my dress," she says.

I release the breath I'd been holding. "I'm good. It's all good." Because this is no longer about Kennedy's list. The list is gone, and she stopped talking to me days ago. This is about me. And Nate.

Assured that I'm not going to make a fool of either one of us, Cousin Pen heads off toward a group of Cupcakes. The large room, aglow with only twinkle lights and candles, holds at least a thousand students. An entire wall of glass overlooks the ocean, and somewhere on that ocean is a twenty-five-foot boat with a teak deck and dolphin bobblehead, and when Nate takes that boat out next summer, I want to be on it.

Shoeless, I walk the perimeter, squinting through the semi-darkness for dark hair and dimples. I picture Nate in his proper and perfect prom attire: black tuxedo, shiny black shoes, and raven-wing hair, every bit of him oozing charm and confidence.

Hundreds of students crowd the dance floor, and I zigzag through the dancers, tapping shoulders and nudging people out of the way in my search for Nate. On my second swing around the floor, the emcee announces the senior prom court. The queen is a girl with orange-red hair and red platform shoes with laces and a tassel, like something out of a 1940s movie. The guy wears a cute scarf.

Nate is nowhere to be seen. I rush outside and search the patio and fire pit area. I try the rooftop lookout. I even scour the parking lot, searching for his dad's truck. No Nate. But he has to be here, because he's a prom kind of guy.

Back inside the ballroom, I go on another Nate hunt, and when I don't find him, I head for the only place I haven't looked. On the way to the men's bathroom I spot a familiar buzz cut atop no neck near one of the food and beverage stations. I run to Bronson and grab his arm. "Where's Nate?"

Bronson, who holds a plate of mini meatballs and mozzarella sticks, looks at me and squints. "Rebel?"

I smooth my hand along the sea-glass hair clip. "Yep, I clean up pretty good. Now where's Nate?"

Bronson pops a meatball into his mouth. "He's not coming."

"What? He's supposed to be here with a girl from his calculus class."

"Something came up with her family, and she had to cancel."

"And he didn't ask anyone else?"

"No."

"Isn't he coming alone?"

"He sold his ticket."

"That makes no sense." I clutch his arm. "Prom is important to him. He should be here." My words are loud and panicky.

Bronson leans in. "Have you been drinking?"

"No." I nudge him away. "Nor am I doing drugs." I tap the broken shoes against my thigh. What now? I didn't come for the mozzarella sticks. I don't want to dance and stand in circles chatting about summer plans. I want Nate.

I spin around—and smack into a bronze brick wall.

"Where have you been?" Nate's words are snappish and breathy, as if he's been running. But he's not dressed for running. Nor is he dressed for prom. He wears shorts, a white tank, and flip-flops. A sloppy wing of hair hangs over his forehead, and I have a crazy urge to run my fingers through it. "Gabby said you were supposed to be with Penelope and her friends."

"I've been running around looking for *you*," I say. "Where have you been?"

"Running around looking for you." He grabs my arm and pulls me toward the door. "Mission accomplished. Now we need to get going."

I dig my heels in. "Wait, what are you doing?"

"Getting you out of here."

"Why? This is prom."

He pushes his hair off his forehead, but it falls back. "You don't belong here."

The panic swirls in my chest. No. He's wrong. This conversation is wrong. "Listen, Nate. I'm trying. Don't you see I'm trying?" I raise my hands in a pleading gesture, and the broken heel falls to the floor. I grab it and tuck the wounded shoes behind my back. "I can do this. I can be a normal girl at a normal dance. For you."

"No, Reb. I'm serious. You don't belong *here*." I open my mouth, but he presses a finger to my lips. "And neither do I." For the first time tonight, Nate's dimples appear, and all of a sudden things seem very, very right.

Heads spin as Nate hustles me out the door. It's a good thing I've been working out with the track team for weeks, or I'd be struggling to match his pace as we hurry along the boardwalk. I don't ask where we're going, because Nate, as usual, has everything under control, or, at least, I hope he does. There's something different about him tonight, something a little less buttoned-up.

Tonight the moon hangs full and low, the sky glowing with false twilight that illuminates Nate's face. His hint of a smile grows to a full-fledged grin by the time we reach the marina. He waves to the guard at the security booth and leads me along the crisscrossing docks lined with boats of every shape and size. I picture Nate's face the day he told me about the twenty-five-foot Hunter sailboat with teak deck and bobble-head dolphin. I saw joy mingled with longing and a dash of adventure. He wears the same look now, but to the tenth power.

Midway down a dock, he turns me toward the water and motions to a boat with a grand sweep of his arm. "Beautiful, isn't she?"

"She's . . ." I press my lips together, trying to keep a straight face. "She's something, all right." I know very little about boats, but this tiny sailboat is no sleek, twenty-five-foot Hunter with a teak deck that will make it all the way to the Baja.

"She's a twelve-footer, a 1974 Montgomery, and she's mine."

"You bought this boat?"

"Technically, I'm still buying it." He takes the shoes from my hand and flings them into the bottom of the boat. "I took the money that I would have spent on prom—money for a tux, dinner, flowers, the tickets—and used it to put a down payment on this. The former owner is going to let me make payments every week, and, come the end of summer, she'll be paid off and all mine."

"I'm happy for you Nate. I really am." He's listening to his heart and honoring his true self, and I can see it on his face.

He squeezes my hand. "Me, too." Then he lets out a quick breath. "Now it's time."

"For what?"

His dimples deepen. "The anti-prom."

I laugh. "The what?"

"You'll see." He puts one foot into the boat and reaches for my hand. I lift my skirt to climb in, but he shouts, "Wait!" He drops my hand and leaps into the boat without a sound, all strength and agility and grace. Still a sporto at heart. He fumbles with a box at the front end, and seconds later, soft violin music floats on the air. Then he reaches into his pocket, takes out a book of matches, and lights a tiny candle with some saintly guy's picture on it.

I picture his sister playing the music and his little saintly brother offering one of his candles, and a lump rises in my throat. "It's beautiful."

He reaches for my hand but then smacks his head. "No! Not yet. Man, I'm screwing this up." With an intense seriousness, he reaches into his pocket and takes out a white bow tie and slips it around his neck. Finally, he takes my hand and escorts me onto his sailboat. On one of the bench seats sits a tray with two sandwiches, a single apple, and two bobbing mounds of flan with a shiny brown sauce.

"Mateo said you really need to try flan with caramel sauce. It's traditional and his best."

I can't speak.

Nate's fingers worry the right side of his hair. "I know it's not normal and—"

"No!" I hold up a hand and add more softly, "No, it's perfect." Like Nate. Like everything about this strange and wonderful night. I have flowers from Uncle Bob, a barrette from Aunt

Evelyn, Cousin Pen's broken shoes, cover-up from Macey, and Percy's penny. My life is far from perfect, and it will never be perfect, but right now, being here at this moment, surrounded by these things, is the right choice.

I've made choices, and I am exactly where I need to be, when I need to be there. With a giddy laugh, I sit on the middle bench, and Nate moves to the back of the boat and starts the engine.

He unhooks the tether and pushes off from the dock. "Time for the ol' *Rebel Girl* to sail."

"*Rebel Girl?*" I dip my head in a not-so-humble bow. "I'm flattered that you're naming your boat after me."

Nate aims the boat toward the open ocean. "Nope. She had the name long before me."

"Come on, Nate."

Nate points to the back of the boat. "Take a look."

I bunch my wispy skirt in my hands and walk to the back of the boat on bare feet. Written across the back in faded letters are the words *Rebel Girl*.

Yes, this is where I belong. I sink back onto the seat, my skirt fanning out like a silvery cloud. I turn my face to the midnight sky, to the stars, to whatever is beyond. Tonight, it all feels right and good.

It's destiny, I say.

Every inch of my skin prickles, and I grab the sides of the boat. It's too dark to see, but I can't help but search for a perky blond ponytail.

ACKNOWLEDGMENTS

This story was born in the aftermath of three deaths that profoundly changed my life and the lives of people I love. To the three who died, thank you for making this world a better place. Joy and peace on your respective journeys.

ABOUT THE AUTHOR

Young adult author Shelley Coriell writes stories about teens on the edge of love, life-changing moments, and a little bit of crazy. Her debut, *Welcome, Caller, This Is Chloe*, was a 2012 Indie Next Pick, and *Publishers Weekly* praised Coriell for her "sparkling wit and great skill in creating complex characters with memorable personalities." You can find Shelley at shelley-coriell.com and on Twitter @ShelleyCoriell.

Also by Shelley Coriell

Welcome, Caller, This Is Chloe

This book was designed by Maria T. Middleton. The text is set in 10.5-point Glypha Light, a geometric slab-serif designed by Adrian Frutiger in 1977. The display fonts are Gotham Light and La Carte Regular.

This book was printed and bound by Worzalla in Stevens Point, Wisconsin. Its production was overseen by Rachel Poloski and Kathy Lovisolo.